RESTITUTION

Richard S. Wheeler

A SIGNET BOOK

SIGNET
Published by New American Library, a division of
Penguin Putnam Inc., 375 Hudson Street,
New York, New York 10014, U.S.A.
Penguin Books Ltd, 27 Wrights Lane,
London W8 5TZ, England
Penguin Books Australia Ltd,
Ringwood, Victoria, Australia
Penguin Books Canada Ltd, 10 Alcorn Avenue,
Toronto, Ontario, Canada M4V 3B2
Penguin Books (N.Z.) Ltd, 182–190 Wairau Road,
Auckland 10, New Zealand

Penguin Books Ltd, Registered Offices:
Harmondsworth, Middlesex, England

First published by Signet, an imprint of New American Library,
a division of Penguin Putnam Inc.

First Printing, February 2001
10 9 8 7 6 5 4 3 2 1

Chapter 1

The three forks of Cottonwood Creek purled out of the foothills as sweet and clear as the Gospel and gathered together just above the town of Cottonwood, which called itself thrice blessed. Of all of life's benefactions, water was the most important. And cool, crystal water was a blessing beyond compare. For Cottonwood, snugged comfortably on the south flank of the Uinta Mountains, sweet cold water meant prosperous ranches, green fields, healthy cattle, good business in the dry-goods and grocery stores, and comfort. It was a place to sink roots.

Each winter heaped snows in layers fifty feet thick in the blue mountain canyons, and each summer these sun-chastened snows fed the three forks, giving a timeless rhythm to the area, and preserving it for the happy few who had found it to be a veritable promised land. Herefords and shorthorns and a few of the old longhorns dotted the creek banks, drinking deep on hot summer days, and wandering off to golden slopes filled with sun-cured bunchgrass to fatten and grow.

The people in that vicinity considered the water a metaphor for the life they lived there. This was not fouled water, full of mortal sin and brimming with man's vices, but new and clean and virtuous water. This was not alkaline water, twisting body and soul. This was pure water, like grace, like heaven, and like innocence.

The citizens of Cottonwood proudly said that the water had no taste at all, for there were no impurities to season it. A few swore they tasted pine and sky and wildflowers in it, but they were being fanciful. The sober, considered verdict in Cottonwood was that this water was clean as an unborn soul, and as health-giving as the best efforts of all the world's doctors.

Cottonwood had sprung up as a crossroads in the seventies, soon after the earliest cattlemen arrived and staked out the various valley bottoms for their ranches. Now, in the mid-eighties, it was a well-established and pleasant county seat that had cast off its rude origins and set itself to the twin tasks of achieving virtue and prosperity.

Far up the South Fork, on land more arid, tilted, and stony than the country below, lived a young couple who were among the last to settle in the district. But the water was just as fine there as below. Maybe finer. They had arrived with nothing, and after scouting the area, they had homesteaded, worked at odd jobs, persevered, bought newly patented land, and gradually cobbled together a fine ranch. But it was one that required more care and effort than the lower ranches, where the

Elysian fields seemed to care for themselves and the cattle upon them.

Truman Jackson and his wife Gracie didn't mind the extra toil or the longer trip to town. They had snatched up the last suitable country and built a stout ranch upon it that rivaled those below for the fatness of its stock and the abundance of its hay lands. It had something the lower ranches lacked, which was a breathtaking prospect in every direction. The Jacksons had taken advantage of it by setting their log house at just the angle so that every window opened upon paradise.

As for the extra labor, weren't they raising two husky boys and a dutiful girl to help out? In town, knowing people said that the Jackson place was going to last for generations. And Truman and Gracie often echoed the same sentiment. Having found Eden, they had set out to put their TJ brand on it.

The Jacksons were much admired in Cottonwood, not only because they were a handsome and gregarious family, but because Truman took to ranching with uncanny skill, as if he were driven by some interior demon, and succeeded in an area where other men may have faltered. Truman was active in Grange affairs, and his views were carefully weighed by his neighbors. He wrestled with ways to beat the great packing plants that dictated the price paid for beef on the hoof, and with the railroads whose rates punished stockmen, grossly reducing the value of their livestock.

One could expect the Jacksons at any potluck dinner, or any of the town's holiday celebrations, or at the annual caroling at Christmas. They were friendly, but there was something odd about them, and people noticed it. They seemed to have no past. They talked little about their families, or wherever they had grown up, or relatives, or states and towns and counties back East.

To make matters even more peculiar, Gracie in particular spun a dozen conflicting stories about her childhood. Had she grown up in Maine, Missouri, or Michigan? Was she an only child, or one of three sisters, or one of seven children? Had her father been a cobbler, or a salesman, or a sea captain? Had her mother run a hotel or a restaurant, or had she died when Gracie was very young?

And as for Truman, he simply smiled and turned silent. When pressed, he said he had come from humble origins and had made his way in the world from a tender age, nine to be exact, somehow surviving wherever he could but always on the frontier.

And so the citizens of Cottonwood let the matter drop. No one wished to be nosy; the Jacksons were valued neighbors, solid and well-off ranchers, active in town, good hosts to many friends. So what did it matter that no mail from their families ever arrived, and no brothers or sisters, parents or grandparents, ever rode into Cottonwood for a visit?

One other thing about the Jacksons occasioned much gossip at the time it happened. For the first two years of their life in Cottonwood, they chose no church and did not seem likely to, expressing no interest in religion or even understanding of it. Then, after they had their ranch in operation, they turned timidly toward the Community Church, an amalgam of several Protestant denominations, attending the Sunday services now and then.

Eventually, they sought to become members, and only then did it come out, to everyone's surprise, that they had never been baptized. Just as astonishingly, neither of them had the faintest grasp of doctrine, or had ever read so much as a chapter of the Bible. All this came to light when the Reverend Mr. Eli Pickrell routinely questioned them about matters of faith before admitting them to the congregation.

The upshot of all that was that for the better part of a year, Truman and Gracie Jackson, along with Nell, Jon, and Parker, received instruction in Sunday school preceding the regular services. Truman and Gracie were the only adults in a class of a dozen stair-step children. Cottonwood buzzed with that oddity, but approved. How could it not find the gathering of two ignorant sheep into the fold agreeable?

Those who had a good ear could sometimes hear revealing things in Gracie's language. She had not grown up in gentle or proper surroundings; the cognoscenti were sure of that. Coarse figures of speech sometimes slipped from her in moments when she was off guard, and then she either ignored them or attempted to wallpaper over the offense with a little laugh. "I used to shock my mother, just to be a naughty girl," she would say, and go on to other things.

But the upright citizens of Cottonwood really didn't mind. The Jacksons were well accepted, the doors of the best homes were open to them, and whatever their backgrounds, they had transcended their origins.

But there were other things that a few of the shrewder citizens of Cottonwood had noticed. Truman Jackson sometimes slid into periods of deep silence, and at least one of his neighbors thought that Truman was afraid of something. He never entered a room without seeming to be looking for someone, passing the time of day by studying each passerby, or sweeping the horizon with his gaze, as if expecting a horseman to appear out of the woods.

He seemed to be a man acquainted with danger, and some of the town's gossips were certain that Jackson had once been a soldier. Too young for the Civil War, but not for the Indian campaigns that followed. The old habits of a military man in the field had not left Jackson. Or so they reasoned, and with good sense.

And yet they never knew for sure. Once someone asked Truman whether he had served, and he had only smiled and shook his head. He remained a mystery, but the townspeople knew that as the years passed, the Jacksons would eventually share their pasts with their neighbors.

In 1882, some of the town's leading citizens formed the Cottonwood State Bank and invited

Truman Jackson to join the board of directors. But Jackson politely declined, pleading distance and the press of work. He did offer to open an account there, though, and use the bank's resources when he was trading or buying or selling livestock.

That was quite understandable. Jackson's ranch was an hour's ride from town on a fast saddler, and two hours by wagon.

Sheriff Styles Quail had once asked Jackson to be a part of a special posse he was forming for emergencies, but Jackson had declined, saying that he wasn't much of a man with small arms, and had but one, a rusty Colt he kept around to put a horse or cow out of its misery.

All that was true enough. Jackson didn't wear a side arm, unlike some of the ranchers in the Cottonwood district. Rustling happened from time to time, and drifters had often wandered through the area, which was why some ranchers felt a need to stay heeled. Cottonwood was not free of crime, but the sheriff's pursuit of law and order usually involved no more than coping with schoolboys' pranks and the rowdiness of cowboys on payday.

One summer, when a newcomer built a two-story saloon on the west edge of town and began catering to the local drovers, supplying not only spirits and gambling tables, but—it was rumored—a couple of doxies who occupied the second floor, the locals grew indignant. The women of Cottonwood circulated a petition to have ordinances passed suppressing this sort of thing.

They buttonholed Gracie one day when she was

buying ribbons at Smith's, and insisted she sign.
But her response was distinctly odd. What were the
names of the girls? Who was the new saloon man?
Where were they from?

The townswomen were taken aback. They ex-
plained that they didn't know or care. But Gracie
signed anyway, slowly, pensively, her thoughts a
thousand miles distant.

All these oddities seemed to interest no one except the postmaster, Horatio Bates, who studied the
Jacksons with mounting curiosity year after year,
although the Jacksons were utterly unaware of it.
And Bates had gradually formed some startling
conclusions.

Chapter 2

Each and every day, Truman Jackson wrestled with the most painful decision of his life. For over a year he had fought the same battles in his soul, back and forth, without ever committing to action. He wondered how it would end, and whether he would find the courage if he did decide to act.

Gracie was so horrified she refused even to listen to him whenever he broached that dread topic. She simply compressed her lips and fled the room. Earlier, the very mention of the idea wrought tears from her blue eyes. He was on his own. He would do what he had to do, or not do anything at all.

He did not lack happiness, and his torment did not rise from misery. Indeed, he was happier and more content than he ever dreamed he might be. He had the esteem of all of Cottonwood: friends, intimates, fine strapping boys, a sugar-and-spice daughter, a fruitful land that had yielded its wealth, fat cattle, trust—that somehow amazed him—and honor. Above all, he had Gracie, who had shared everything, knew every secret of the dark corners of his heart, and had walked together with him from beginnings so distant and dark that even now, that long journey astonished him. He could not have done it alone.

He had contentment, too. Ambition wasn't a bottomless pit that he could never fill. He didn't need more money, he didn't yearn for a prettier wife, or more children, or more power and prestige in Cottonwood. He had enough of the important things. But he knew he must grow. All of us must grow or shrink, because our souls never stand still. There were areas where it was best to be ever discontent, and one of those is shaping one's character into something finer, stronger, more loving, more tender, and more honest. Only in that realm of spirit and heart was Truman Jackson discontent. And that surprised him as much as his entire life surprised him. This was the thinking of a new man.

He could not quite fathom what had started the young man he had once been toward this life. He had once been an entirely different man, hard and bitter, hungry and angry, his hatreds seething just under a false calm that existed only to keep him out of trouble. Had God's finger touched him? How could he answer a question like that? God confused him still. And now, he was sure, God's finger was touching him again, and had been for a year or so, driving him to distraction.

This morning, like so many others, he was thinking about the dilemma he faced, and wondering if he had acquired any new insight. He knew he hadn't. This battle was one he had fought and refought in his mind so many times he knew the secrets of each army as it marched across his heart. He wished he could talk more to Gracie; he wanted to carry her with him on this journey, share this ordeal, and this triumph, if it came to that.

The mornings were always chilly at that altitude, even on a summer's day. He liked to get up before dawn, which at this time of year meant rising at five. He ritually built a small fire in the big Majestic, filled a blue-speckled coffeepot with water he dippered from a bucket, and set it on the range to heat up while he ground some Arbuckle's Best. Now, a steaming cup of java in hand, he headed out to his porch to behold the sunrise on the mountains, a wonderment that never failed to whisper to him of the goodness of the world and the certitude that the earth and moon and sun were still whirling in their trajectories and always would be. Some things endured.

Dew lay thick on the grass and glistened along the tops of fence rails. A stillness lay over the land, a sacred hush before the world began sinning in earnest. The somber flanks of the Uintas slowly turned amber, then golden, and finally creamy under the paintbrush of the awakening sun. Jackson heard his household stirring. He had children to feed and nurture, a wife to love and support, a homestead to protect. And if his conscience drove him to do what he had to do, he would hurt them all, sear them with fire, branding them and ruining their lives forever.

He heard Gracie in the kitchen. The pungence of the coffee always awakened her. The fresh hot

Brazil grind was his daily gift to her. She poured a cup and drank it slowly before doing anything else.

He discovered her at the rail beside him. She had pulled her ash hair back and wrapped a purple ribbon about it. She wore a shapeless gray cotton dress, and he knew she would soon be tackling a tough project, such as scrubbing the plank floors. What lay under that dress still ignited explosions in him, as it had when they were wild and in trouble and living from minute to minute. They had met in a distant place, as far away from here as they could get with what little they had. She had run with him, and become someone else with him. But those were different times, wild and bitter.

"You're thinking about it again," she said.

"Yes."

She sighed unhappily. This fencing had gone on so long that it no longer played out in words. They each knew the script.

"I wish I could just be secure. Just believe that we'll be here tomorrow, a month from now, next year. That's what I did believe until you got this in your head."

He nodded. In the past he had assured her that nothing would change, but now he no longer made the argument. She didn't believe it, and there was no point in asserting it.

"It's like a shadow has been cast over this home," she said. "Like the wing of an owl. I feel so helpless. You'll do what you'll do, and pay me no heed."

At first he had denied this accusation, but now

he saw it was a harsh truth. If he went ahead, he would be paying her no heed.

He and Gracie had known each other since he was seventeen and she was sixteen. Now he was thirty-four. It had been a long, winding trail, along precipices, across raging rivers, atop ridges, into box canyons where they had to turn around, but eventually it led them to this place—and this state of mind. The latter was truer than the former. The trail they had walked in such pain wasn't merely a geographical one, but a spiritual odyssey that drained one sort of life out of them and replaced it with another.

Along the way he had abandoned the name he was given, but she hadn't. Truman Jackson was an invented name, and one he had given much thought to. The temptation had been to use his old initials, or keep his first name and merely alter the last, or come close to the way his other name sounded. In the end he rejected all those notions and chose a name that could not be linked in any way to his former one. But Gracie had always been Gracie; she merely adopted his new surname as her own, when they crossed that bridge one night fleeing for their lives across snowy slopes. It was more likely that someone would recognize her than him, because he had been so young and so invisible, so gaunt and dour that people had always given him wide berth.

But she had been well-known in Fort Benton, and a hundred lustful men a year had sought her favors, from the very day she began to bud. But if she had inherited anything from her mother, it was a way with men, and she had, from about thirteen onward, laughed them off. All of them, except for Will Dowd, the boy who had become Truman Jackson.

Fort Benton was a wild place in those days, just before the transcontinental railroad began to shut down the traffic on the Missouri River. Fort Benton had been the gateway to the northwest for over a decade. Each spring, riding snowmelt from the distant Rockies, the paddle wheel boats burdened with supplies and restless men had toiled up the Missouri to Benton, the head of navigation not far from the Great Falls of the Missouri, and then spread out upon the wilderness of the Territory of Montana. Good men and bad. Good women and bad. But mostly men.

Gracie's mother ran a boardinghouse in Fort Benton. She had run other boardinghouses in other feral places. She liked wild times and wild men, one of whom had sired Gracie sometime, somewhere. Truman didn't know where or who, only how.

Gracie's mother was not a woman in a disreputable profession and had never been. But she would not have been very welcome in the parlor of any parsonage. Whenever Kid Dowd, Truman's uncle, lingered in Fort Benton, he stayed at the boardinghouse, and so did Truman, who at that time was still known as Will. And so did the other four, the Dillin boys, Rufe, Gin, Monk, and Slam. They were Will's cousins. Altogether they num-

bered six, but Will, who was youngest and merely
held horses, did not get a full share. He got half a
share, and so did Slam, the youngest of the Dillin
boys, who functioned as lookout.

The authorities thought that the Dillin-Dowd
gang had only four men at the core, though the
numbers varied over the years. Will had never
known another life. His father had been killed robbing the Laramie-Deadwood stage, and then Kid
Dowd became father in name, if not fact. Will
Dowd had grown up on the lam. Unlike more notorious gangs, this one kept quiet, stayed out of saloons, and tried to put something away for the day
when everything went wrong. It preyed upon the
stage lines between Fort Benton, Helena, and Virginia City. It held up Concord coaches in the stretch
between Columbus and Livingston. Kid Dowd, its
leader, was a polite and melancholy bandit, addressing ladies courteously even while extracting
rings, bracelets, necklaces, and cash from them. The
gang was credited with thirty-seven robberies, and
suspected in four others, throughout Montana Territory and Wyoming.

They switched to bullion now and then for diver-
sion, and that was when the Dillin-Dowd Gang got
into trouble.

They ambushed a stagecoach at Wolf Creek,
knowing it carried Helena gold but not knowing it
carried a shotgun messenger inside the coach. The
response was not swift surrender, but swifter bul-
lets. One killed Kid Dowd, others wounded two of
the Dillin boys. The gang returned the fire, but the

jehu urged his four spans of mules into a fast trot down the canyon and escaped.

But for a price. The Fort Benton *River Press* reported that a widow coming to town to open a restaurant lost every cent. A storekeeper had been gravely injured and clung to life at Fort Shaw. The jehu lost an eye. A little boy had been so frightened that he had slid into dementia.

The gang had been recognized, but not Will, seventeen, back a hundred yards on Wolf Creek, holding the pack mules that were to carry the bullion, and three spare saddlers just in case. No one had ever known about Will Dowd and no one ever would. Except Gracie.

Chapter 3

The flight was blurred but the odyssey wasn't. Truman Jackson couldn't remember much of that first year of escape, a year of looking over his shoulder and studying every ranch, farm, town, and person he came across. But he remembered exactly how he had been transformed.

After the trouble, he had sneaked back to Fort Benton, studied the boardinghouse for an hour from behind the privy, and then waited until the lamps went out. He knew how to reach Gracie's little room on the second floor; he had come to her several times before by crawling up a shed roof. He was the first and only boy she had ever held in her arms. She would not be startled when he tapped lightly on her window.

"Will?" she whispered.

"Get dressed. You're coming with me."

"But, Will—"

"Shhh. Are they looking for me?"

"Looking? No. Why—"

"You've got to come."

She had stared at him, making up her mind.

Then slowly she slipped out from under her comforter, and Will had been dizzy with desire, but he simply stood and waited, crazy about Gracie, proud that she loved him. She was his girl. He had been in this little room several times, once all night. His heart lifted when she stuffed her things into a pillow slip and the rest into a gunny sack. Minutes later they had tiptoed down the creaking stairs and into the bleak night. He had a horse and a pack mule. They had loaded her stuff on the pack mule behind his war bag, and then quietly slipped from Fort Benton.

He remembered that much. The rest was a haze.

They could not ford the Missouri River, and could not wake up the ferryman to head south into a prairie wilderness still haunted by Crow and Blackfoot, so he steered west along the river road. It would take them around the Great Falls of the Missouri and then into the mountains, along the very route that would lead them to the scene of the attempted stagecoach robbery, and the ensuing disaster.

But they saw no one.

They spent the first days arguing about everything—where to go, what to do, where to find food. He had worried that one of the gang had squealed and now the lawmen were looking for him.

The memories of those days simply eluded him now. He and Gracie had found odd jobs, made love, camped well off the trails, swam in the frigid night air in the cold Missouri until their teeth chattered. They had avoided Helena, worked awhile around Townsend, and finally found themselves in the vast and beautiful Gallatin Valley, surrounded by snowcapped mountains. They were still drifting south and west, and he was still looking behind him every few seconds while she watched somberly. Gracie was having regrets. Rough living, without the smallest comfort, was eroding her will to go on.

There, in that mountain-girt valley, he had changed his name, talked to her about beginnings, persuaded her that things would get better fast, and asked her to be his wife.

They had married themselves. He didn't know the words to any ceremony; he had never even been in a church. So he told her he wanted her for a wife, forever, and she said she wanted him forever, and that was that. Sometimes, when she was warm and they weren't afraid of being found, she took him eagerly. Most of the time, Gracie turned aside and told him to wait.

He didn't like to wait. He didn't like anything that thwarted him. He had a temper. He was suspicious whenever she was out of sight. He lived with a mortal fear boiling in him. He approached no strangers, and whenever he scented danger he turned sharply away. She was growing impatient with him, with the drifter's life, with hunger and cold and grime.

"Gracie, just wait until we're out of Montana, out of Wyoming, somewhere else. Just wait."

She had stared, somberly.

Now he remembered the thousands of places, the

ranches where they would work before drifting on, the deer and antelope he shot to stay alive, which neither of them knew how to butcher. But if he were pressed now to trace their route on a map, or name the places, he knew he could not do it.

But he could do something else. Another side of that flight he remembered vividly. For he had entered it as an outlaw boy, cynical and bitter, afraid and angry, mean and tender. A year later those things were, at best, shadows. In the space of a year, his soul had been transformed.

He had grown up thinking work was for suckers. If you want something, pull out your six-gun and take it. But during that long, confused flight, he and Gracie had worked hard. He didn't want trouble, or to call attention to himself. So he did whatever needed doing. He split kindling, cut firewood, shocked hay, unloaded boxcars, mucked stalls in livery barns, delivered packages, built fences, and whitewashed buildings. Gracie had mostly cooked and waited tables.

He hated it at first, doing as little as possible, and often encountered frowns and resistance when it came time to settle. But then one day, in some town he couldn't remember, he had worked hard cutting jack pine into stove wood, angrily whacking away because his life was going nowhere and he was tired of this toil. Unwittingly he cut more than the cord he had bargained for, and when he had stacked the wood beside the ranch kitchen, the old gent who ran the place pulled out a tape measure, studied the pile to make sure it was four feet by four feet by eight, and suddenly smiled.

"Well over a cord. Cord and a third, I reckon. Here's the five, and an extry two dollars, and if you want to cut more, you're welcome to do it. You're a good and true man, Jackson, and better than your word. The world needs more like you."

Jackson had stared at the seven silver dollars in his hand, amazed. He had been given a forty-percent bonus for a third more wood.

Up until that moment he had imagined everyone he worked for had been trying to euchre him, and he had sullenly entered each transaction ready to quit the instant he suspected he was being cheated.

Now he had two dollars more than he had bargained for, and the offer of more work.

After that he quit worrying about being cheated, and tried to give more than he had bargained for. Sometimes he got extra, sometimes he didn't. But no one complained anymore. Mostly he and Gracie bartered, because cash was so short on the frontier. She cooked and washed dishes for food. He mucked out stalls for baits of grain and hay for his horses. She washed clothing in exchange for some cast-off skirts. He unloaded freight wagons for an old tent and two new bedrolls. He spent a day pumping a blacksmith's bellows in exchange for shoes for his footsore mule.

He had changed through all those months, but so imperceptibly that he didn't realize it until much later. He began to take pride in his work. He liked the moment when he got paid by someone who was satisfied with his labor. He liked being accepted. He discovered, to his amazement, that honest work was easier than living the desperate life of an outlaw. The rage and fear of his former life soon fell away.

Gracie had always worked hard in her mother's boardinghouse, cooking, cleaning, washing linens, doing dishes, sweeping, liming the privy, buying enough food for breakfast and dinner for eight men each and every day. She had never been paid a nickel by her mother, and now she was receiving tangible things for her toil. A dress, a coat, blankets, cash.

Little did Truman Jackson grasp that he was leaving Will Dowd behind, and that he could never turn back. Little did he realize that he was happier and less worried. But he never stopped looking over his shoulder, and in his heart he answered to the name Will, and supposed he always would. One thing he knew: the Dowd gang was a legend wherever men talked about outlaws.

He and Gracie might have drifted for years, putting ever more distance between themselves and Fort Benton when something changed all that. Gracie became pregnant. It was time to stop running. But where would they go, and with what?

Their possessions had multiplied. A year of drifting and working had won them a canvas-covered wagon they had outfitted as a tiny home, a pair of draft horses to pull it, a dairy cow, and ample tools and clothes and bedding.

"I guess we'd better look for a place to settle," he'd said after they had spent the night rejoicing. "A boy needs a home."

"A girl needs one even more," Gracie had retorted.

At that point they were laboring in southwestern Wyoming, around Rock Springs and Evanston.

"Gracie, let's get into Utah," he said. He wanted one more state line between him and the Montana lawmen. The idea seemed foolish. No one was looking for him. No one knew that he had been part of that gang. He and Gracie didn't need to run. But still, Utah was full of quiet people, those Mormons mostly, and he reckoned he would find a quiet town in a quiet valley and live a quiet life.

It was only then that he realized how much he had changed and matured. Now, beginning his nineteenth year, he wondered whether he was still Will Dowd, youngest punk in a robber gang, or whether he was the man whose name he had invented. He was still plenty scared, and had learned a dozen ways to turn conversation away from his and Gracie's past. He heard the name "Will" shouted sometimes, and brutally resisted jerking his head around to see who wanted him. If he was becoming a new man, he had not surrendered the cunning and caution that shielded him from disaster. And neither had Gracie.

They had rolled into sleepy Cottonwood one autumnal afternoon, and turned to each other and smiled.

Chapter 4

Gracie had always stood by her man. Together, she and Truman had walked a path from darkness to light, from ruin to hope. She remembered what they had been: selfish, suspicious, what's-in-it-for-me young people, fleeing iron bars and a record that would hang around Truman's neck all of his days.

Now they were different. She better understood why good was good and evil was evil. She understood why lawmen existed, and laws, and beliefs, and God. Before, all those things had just gotten in the way. Now they nurtured the Jacksons, kept them from hurting others and themselves, and offered them safety.

She had stood by him, but now she wondered if she still could. He was going to do this deed that would tear them apart, destroy everything they had built, threaten their escape from darkness. He was going to spill it all. She could not let him do that. This time she could not stand by her man and let him destroy their world, their children's lives, their dreams, their good name.

It had all started half a year earlier when one fine morning after church, Truman corralled her in his dark and masculine ranch office, redolent of leather and beeswax.

"Gracie, I'm thinking on something . . ."

The tone of voice caught her attention. "Yes?"

"We're still running. We're still hiding. We don't have to do that anymore."

Something cold ballooned in her, and she gripped the Morris chair.

"Gracie, we've changed. Somehow or other, we've become new people. But those who know us don't know my real name. I'm still Will Dowd, and I still ran with the Dillin-Dowd Gang, and I held horses while my older kin robbed stagecoaches and banks and trains. It's not atoned, not forgiven so long as I'm hiding who I am."

"No, Truman, don't talk so."

"But it's true, Gracie. I still walk the streets wondering when some man with a badge is gonna stop me. I still want to tell people this Jackson fellow isn't the real-born person."

"Truman, don't you dare!"

"I've been thinking, Gracie. We have to take the final step. We have to fess up and pay back the people I stole from. I can't pay 'em all, but I can pay some. We've a little to spare."

"But, Truman, that's so long ago. You were seventeen, sixteen. Now we've children and a new life. You'd hurt Nell and Parker and Jon."

"I think they'd get over it, maybe even take pride in it."

"You're putting yourself and me in danger."

"Statute of limitations, Gracie. Ran out long ago. No one's gonna come with a warrant after all these years."

"But we escaped. No one even knew you were part of that gang."

He shrugged. "Lots of kin to talk about it all these years. It's probably known."

Had it been any other proposal to remedy a wrong she would have approved. They had forged new characters out of the dross of their old ones. He stood across from her, filled out into manhood, adult, grave yet smiling, a light in his eyes, serene and secure and calm. Neither of them was above average height, but somehow he seemed tall, arrow-straight, no slouch or weakness in him.

He was better-looking than she. Her blocky figure was her despair. Men said she was curvy, but that was her despair, too. She couldn't even say what there was about her that had attracted the young Will Dowd in the first place. He probably had just been a woman-hungry kid, and she had been just wild enough and loose enough to draw him like a fly to the sugar bowl.

"It's a high-minded thing to think about, but the world is different, Truman. It won't work out like you say."

"I've thought of that. Even if things go bad, even if we are driven out of here, it's something I have to do. Make things right. That's what remorse and repentance are about. Everything has to be made right."

She gulped deeply, freedom's air in a free land. "All our lives we've made decisions together. Everything. We never did anything separately. When one of us didn't approve, that was the end of it. Are you going to change that?"

"Gracie, I've got to do what I've got to do, and make myself whole again. I think old Pickrell would help. He's no fire-eater; he would just tell the congregation not to judge me, but to see what I am now and keep their peace. That's the key to it, Gracie. I'm not that tough kid. People will know that."

But all these arguments cut no ice with her. She shook her head. "And what if it doesn't work? You know what people will really think? We can't trust that man. We can't let him bank with us. We won't give credit to that old bank robber. We won't buy those cattle. Probably mavericked or rustled. We won't let our children befriend those punk kids. . . . That's what they'll think. This is a hard world, even in Cottonwood, Truman."

He grinned. "Call me Will, for a change."

She gaped at him, horrified, and the grin slid away from his face. He stared at her somberly. "I have to resolve this. I won't be a whole man in Cottonwood until everything about me is known to everyone."

"You are a whole man! One of the most respected men in the whole area!"

He stood there, his gaze direct and honest, his heart as big as all the world. She loved him so, and never more than now, when his great heart was leading him still farther along his trail to the stars. He was more of a man than anyone else in Cottonwood because he had been tested. He had lifted himself out of darkness. How many of the others had done that? How many had faced their own temptations and triumphed? How many hid vices behind their good names?

"Truman," she said softly, "I'm so proud of you. No other man in your circumstances would even think of such a thing, or risk so much for the sake of justice and goodness. None!"

"Well, this one more step, Gracie, this last step . . ."

"Would you do this much? Would you think about all this for a while more?"

"Sure, there's no rush. But it has to be done. I want to walk down the street and not be two people."

"Would you think about how you'll do this? I think that's important, too. We need to think of our children and our future."

"It's important for them to know."

"Yes, and maybe you should tell them first. That's what I mean. Do this right if you must. But I just wish you'd let things alone . . ."

"Gracie, let's suppose worse comes to worse. Let's suppose the Jacksons aren't welcome here anymore. Let's suppose that I go broke paying off people whose money the gang stole. Let's suppose we have nothing left, not a cent, not a good name, nothing. But we will still know who we are, and the good we've done, and the road we've traveled.

We both of us believe in the Almighty God, and He'll be with us no matter what else happens."

She sighed shakily, loving him, admiring him, yet slipping into utter confusion. He had never been very practical or realistic. It was she who had ended up making sure they got full measure of cordwood or grain, and that fifty-pound sacks of flour really weighed that much, and that the day labor they sometimes employed wasn't sleeping under a pine tree hidden from sight. His mind had leaped from the boyhood "gimme" to "Take whatever you want. Nothing I possess is that important."

It didn't even bother him that some sharpers were always trying to squeeze an extra dime out of him, reading scales wrong, sending spoiled goods out to the ranch. Cottonwood might be a sleepy and virtuous place, but it had its share of chiselers, and none were worse than livestock dealers and horse traders.

"You know," she said, "you don't have to do this alone. You could seek advice. You could talk to Eli Pickrell first. Just go to the parsonage, make sure you're alone, and then lay your burden before him. He might have very different ideas. He might say, don't make a public issue of this. You've made your peace with God. If you want to begin restitution, you could do it anonymously. Find out who suffered from the gang, and let Mr. Pickrell send the money. Don't you see, Truman?"

He nodded, but seemed reluctant. "That wouldn't

do it. I'd still be hiding. I have to tell everyone in Cottonwood."

She felt defeat sliding through her. He was going to do this regardless of what she thought. "Just please wait, please think of ways to protect the children and me, and please talk to someone you trust. You shouldn't do this all alone."

"I have you."

She nodded, wanting to say yes but unable to.

"Six months?" she asked.

"Sure, Gracie, I'll wait that long."

"Well, damn," she said.

Usually that evoked a laugh. It was her way of reminding him of her days as a girl in a rough boardinghouse, with a mother who liked men and kept a few, of a place without many rules except that boarders had to pay promptly or face immediate eviction.

There wasn't anything about men she didn't know by the age of fourteen. There wasn't any cussword she wasn't familiar with by the age of nine. She knew that men were big, strong, kind and mean, generous and pinchpenny, rivalrous in almost everything, forever hungry, and sometimes amazingly tender just when a woman wouldn't expect them to be.

This time Truman didn't smile. He surveyed her seriously, as if she had given offense, and she knew she had inadvertently nudged him one more step toward his public confession.

"Have you talked to Eli Pickrell?"

"No, I'll do it my way."

That disheartened her. "When?" she asked in a small, tender voice.

"At the church potluck."

"What will you say?"

This time he smiled. "That I'm a reformed robber," he replied.

Chapter 5

His fate would spin out at the potluck supper in the basement of the church that summery Sunday evening. As he loaded Gracie's three rhubarb pies into the buggy, he knew from her silence that she was strung as tightly as barbed wire.

He helped her into the old buggy and held her hand.

"Please forgive me," he said.

She nodded stiffly. He had never before seen the strange haunted look that now inhabited her eyes.

They rode through a late afternoon, dust spinning up from the metal tires of the buggy, saying not a word. It had all been said. The only question had been whether to take the children along. Gracie begged him not to, and he had acceded. So they rode to town alone with their secret, which lay between them on the quilted buggy seat like a canister of grapeshot.

They were a little late; it was never easy to gauge the long trip from the ranch into Cottonwood. Truman dropped a carriage weight and helped Gracie carry in the pies and place them on a groaning trestle table. Pots and platters shot savory aromas into the austere basement. Beans, fresh bread, succulent hams, a rib roast, pies, cakes, cookies, potato salad, lemonade, milk, raspberry tarts, heaped corn, potatoes. Most of the congregation was there. The women busied themselves setting out stacks of plates and silver. Shortly the Reverend Mr. Pickrell would intone a blessing, and then with a whoop the hungry people would plunge in.

Truman corralled the busy minister.

"After dinner, I'd like to speak to this group for a few minutes, Mr. Pickrell."

"Speak? About what?"

"Oh, making myself a better man. Doing what is right. Answering my conscience."

"Well, Truman, that"s odd but it sounds uplifting, and I'm in favor of it. I'll do it."

And so the die was cast. There was no escaping it now. Truman thought it would go fairly well, and willed himself to be calm and enjoy the gathering. He had good friends there: Alonzo and Mabel Staples, Joe Nethercutt, Alvira Bjorn, the Tolands, Mrs. Seaton and her boy Jeff, and dozens of others, including the postmaster, Horatio Bates, who was a confirmed old bachelor and rather eccentric, but a likable man nonetheless.

He heaped food onto his plate and dug in, but poor Gracie was not eating at all, and sat to one side looking pale and troubled.

He could not help it. He could not predict the future. He could only do the one thing he had to do, the thing that would at last bring him peace. If all went well, it would be like getting a sore tooth pulled. And if it didn't, he would face the trouble his own way, and pray that his family would be all right.

The feast passed slowly. People headed back for seconds and thirds. Youngsters were flirting. Children whirled outside into the soft warm dusk. Adults settled on benches and makeshift chairs. Women busied themselves rinsing and washing. Men knotted together to talk about the dry pasture, the price of cows, the gold standard, the flagging markets for Utah beef, and the appearance of a racehorse in Cottonwood in the tow of a man who wanted to run match races and wager on them. That brought both curiosity and some frowns. Gambling was a vice.

Outside, the sky drained itself of light, and a soft darkness settled over Cottonwood, shielding its innocence from a harsher world. People began to pack their dishes and plates, preparing to leave. Truman wondered whether Mr. Pickrell had forgotten.

Then, at last, the good reverend rapped sharply on a glass with a spoon and quieted the multitude.

"You know, this is usually the moment when I give a little benediction and see you good folks off. But Truman Jackson asked me to introduce him. He said he would like to talk a few minutes. I gather also that he wishes to witness to his faith, his love of our Lord, and share that with you."

He nodded Truman forward. Truman walked slowly to the trestle table at one end of the hall, knowing he could still escape this if he wished. Gracie sat quietly, her face an inch from tears.

He had rehearsed this several times, trying out the various ways of telling a shocking story. And none had seemed right, so he had decided just to wing it. He would tell it in whatever fashion it came to him.

He drew himself up to his full height. He guessed that the town's bankers and businessmen found him rough-hewn, but he didn't mind. Ranching wasn't for men with soft hands and gabardine suits. They stood about amiably, most of them looking like they wanted to go home, but ready to spare him five minutes. Well, that was all he needed. He eyed Gracie again. She was white and her hands were clenched together.

"Well, giving witness is one word for it," he said. "But this is more in the nature of taking one final step. And when I've taken this step, I'm not at all sure you'll still be my friends. Some of you, I guess, will just about head for the door as fast as you can. But I'm hoping that we'll be shaking hands again, and that what I have to tell you won't alter your vision of the Truman Jackson you've known here in Cottonwood for what—a dozen years? Something like that."

A certain calm settled over him, and he knew then that he would go through with it.

"This is the story of an odyssey, of a boy becoming a man. I want to talk about that boy for a bit now, and that boy's going to shock you."

"Get on with it, Truman," yelled Hobe Bandig, a neighbor. "A lotta hot air's blowin' tonight."

People laughed.

"I was born with a different name," Truman said. "I was born into a family that lived only for the darkness."

That suddenly quieted them.

"My name once was Will Dowd."

He paused, waiting for a response, but found none.

"The only son of Ace Dowd, bandit, robber, killer . . . and my father."

A silence had descended onto that meeting hall, as still as a grave.

"The Dillin-Dowd Gang," he went on. "That was my family. The Dillin boys, Rufe, Gin, Monk, and Slam, were my cousins. Kid Dowd, its leader, was my uncle."

Now came the hard part. "I was part of that gang as a boy. From my fifteenth to my seventeenth year, I held the horses. The authorities didn't know much about me, or my cousin Slam, who was the lookout. They knew all about the older men, all of them dead or in prison now, mostly in Montana Territory."

He could see the expressions change on the rapt faces around him. Families had huddled together tighter. Men's visages had shifted from good-humored acceptance to stone masks.

"You may remember the day when everything went bad. The gang was trying to rob a stagecoach loaded with gold at Wolf Creek, Montana, but the coach had a shotgun rider aboard, and returned fire. Before it was over two cousins and my uncle were dead; my other two cousins were captured; and only the boy, Will, escaped with some of the horses. That boy never committed another crime. He gathered up his true love and fled Montana, on the lam, looking over his shoulder about once a minute."

Now some of the congregation stirred.

"That boy chose a new name, Truman Jackson, and he and his girl worked honestly at everything they could do, cooking and cleaning, unloading boxcars, building fences. You name it. Something began to happen to them. It felt good to work and earn an honest dollar. The boy, Will, had thought work was for suckers. Will had believed that if you wanted something, you took it because everyone was a crook anyway. But the young Truman discovered that the world is mostly populated by good people. He learned that a good job earns respect. He discovered that most people are loving and kind and forgiving. He discovered that we all make mistakes, and most good people try to set things right and go on."

Truman discovered the Reverend Mr. Pickrell staring, obviously anticipating what might come next.

"We ran for a year, Gracie and I. Gracie is her real name—I'm the only one flying false colors until now. By the end of a year of running, working, discovering the goodness of people, of America, of a new sweet land, we felt ready to join some community and make what we could of an honorable life. We ended up in Cottonwood. I guess you know the rest of that story.

"From the day we arrived here, we sought to live in the way we had chosen. We joined this church, yearning for something to lead us to a better life. We found it here, in the preaching of Mr. Pickrell and your fellowship. We were ignorant. Neither of us had the slightest idea of what makes virtue. Neither of us could have recited the Ten Commandments or told you what the Golden Rule was. Here in this church, and in this good community of Cottonwood, we found our bearings.

"God has rewarded us. We've made friends, have the esteem of our community, have children growing up straight and true."

He paused, searching them.

"But the final step was lacking. And I've been thinking about this for months. Truman Jackson isn't the same as Will Dowd, but he still looks at strangers who wear badges, he still looks over his shoulder. He is two men, seeking to be one.

"That's one thing. The other thing is, Truman Jackson wants to set things right with those hurt by the old gang. Will might have only held horses at age sixteen or seventeen, but he bears some of the guilt. I want to set things right because God wants me to. I want to repay whatever my family can spare to the victims of the gang. I am going to try to find them and return all that I can.

"Now that's my story, and you'll have to come to grips with it. I hope you'll call me Truman and be my friend. But some of you will call me Will, and think no man ever changes or grows, or can be freed from the darkness of his past. That's up to you. I have told you all this, before God and man, to make myself whole, and to begin a repayment. That's all I have to say."

They stared at him with uncertainty. Even the reverend gaped, and no one moved.

Chapter 6

Horatio Bates, postmaster of Cottonwood, sat transfixed. He thought that Truman Jackson was a man of exceptional courage. Not only did Jackson reveal what he had been, but he wished to make amends. Nothing had been threatening him. He could have gone to his grave with his secret intact. Yet there he was, slowly intoning his revelations, while the congregation listened, agog.

What sort of man was this? What had inspired this young rancher to speak up? Was he plagued by guilt? Was he still fearful of apprehension? The more Bates listened, the more he realized that neither of these motives applied. Truman Jackson was confessing his past because he felt it was the right and honorable thing to do, and because it was a final step in restoring himself to the world.

Here was one man in a million, the courageous one who set aside all practical considerations—how well Jackson knew what might result from this—because he chose to answer to something higher, finer, truer than mere practicality.

Bates rebuked himself for not having guessed.

He had noticed that the Jacksons received no mail from anywhere else. No family postcard, nothing from friends, no letters postmarked in mysterious and distant places. Only local mail and bills. That had, on occasion, puzzled Bates. He did not lack curiosity, and wherever he held his office as deliverer of the United States mail, he gradually sorted out the town's citizens by their mail. It always amazed him, the things he discovered just by examining return addresses. He knew where people were from, what companies they dealt with, who their relatives were.

Even as Jackson was elaborating a life of redemption, Bates was examining the congregation. The way people were listening told him much. Mrs. Sitgreaves, her lips pursed downward, would never speak to the Jacksons again. Bill Howell was puzzled and unable to make up his mind. Howell was going to sway in whatever direction the crowd swayed. Minerva Constance Welsh, however, wiped her eyes. She was the most generous and forgiving of all the women of Cottonwood, and was always sending some of her spare teaching salary to people in need, a one-woman philanthropy.

But over on the far wall, Hamlin Henshaw lurked, squinting hard, his face granitic. Henshaw was a sheriff's deputy. Nearby stood Grange president Red Bork, who was close to that vulpine old rancher Weber Heeber, absorbing every word in order to use it against Jackson in some devious and rotten way.

Jackson would not escape unscathed.

Then it ended. No one knew what to do or say.

As if awakening from a nightmare, the Reverend Mr. Pickrell cleared his throat.

"That was, ah, a fine witness. We shall see you anon."

Plainly, the reverend wanted to say as little as possible.

Bates sat and waited. He wanted to see who would embrace the Jacksons, and who would not. Scarcely anyone did, save Minerva Welsh, who shook hands with Truman. Bill Howell contemplated it, and then fled, joining his banker friend Bob Scott. Mrs. Sitgreaves ostentatiously and theatrically walked straight past Jackson, plucked up her shawl, and left.

At the last, half a dozen people clustered around the Jacksons. Forty or fifty slid away through the double doors and into a summer's night. One of the last to leave was Hamlin Henshaw, who seemed to be weighing various options.

Bates knew what Henshaw was going to do: he was going to drop in on Sheriff Styles Quail.

It had not gone well for Truman Jackson, but maybe after people had a chance to process all this, things would go better. Bates stood, stretched, and approached the Jacksons.

"That was a courageous and honorable act, Truman."

"It was something I had to do. I'm very grateful that Gracie's still with me."

"Why did you do it?"

Jackson's eyes seemed to gaze off toward distant horizons.

"Oh, it's been building in me."

"No, I mean what inspired it?"

"There are times, Horatio, where a man has to do what he has to do."

"Was it religion?"

"Yes, some."

"Was it a new sense of civic obligation, citizenship?"

"Some."

Bates was perplexed, and enthralled. "Whatever it was, it was the bravest thing I've ever seen. You know, this sort of thing interests me, always has. I'm always looking for people to admire, and you're one."

"Horatio, when a man's done wrong—even as a boy—he's not complete until he sets things right. When I'm done reimbursing those who have claims against me, then I'll be complete. I'm hoping maybe God'll take notice and spare me and my family a good life."

"What if that doesn't happen, Truman?"

"We'll take each day as it comes."

"What if—to take the worst case—you're no longer welcome in Cottonwood?"

"I don't think it'll go that far. People make mistakes. I did, but I also grew up not knowing any better. My father was raising me up to be a predator. But I overcame that. And thanks to Gracie here, we both tried hard to be good neighbors. I think this'll pass. Maybe a few, like one woman here who was glaring daggers at me, maybe those people will look the other way when I come by. But these are good people, and I expect in the end to be welcomed. Cottonwood's our home and we intend to stay, raise our family, ranch, and live our lives the best we can."

"I admire your optimism, Truman. Well, if you ever want to come talk, I've always got a pot of coffee on the stove."

"I might take you up on it, Horatio."

"And one thing more. People are always writing postmasters asking about the character and reputation of someone or other. I just want to tell you that if I ever get a question like that, I'll just let 'em know you're the finest man in Cottonwood."

"Thank you. I don't deserve that."

"I mean it, Truman." Bates turned to Gracie. "And I admire you, too. You'll weather this. You're his strong right arm, Gracie."

She didn't smile. Bates knew, suddenly, that this had torn her to bits.

He headed into the night, elevated by what he had witnessed. Did these people know what they were witnessing? An act of manhood so fine, so clean, so sublime, that they probably would never see the like again?

Bates headed into the quiet town, down dark streets lit by an occasional kerosene lamp in a window. Worry afflicted him. Narrow-minded people were going to make life hard for a man who had just proved himself to be the finest in the county.

The postmaster approached the courthouse and

paused. A light burned, as always, in the sheriff's bailiwick. Quail wouldn't be on duty on a Sunday night, but one deputy would. Bates slipped through shadows until he could peer into the window, but he was too low and could see only the dimly lit ceiling. Then someone approached the window, and yes, it was Deputy Henshaw, talking a blue streak to someone out of sight, probably Max Pink, another of the three deputies. Bates paused and waited, but whoever else was in that office didn't appear at the window.

They were talking about Truman Jackson.

Bates began calculating. Yes, that gang had operated years earlier, and no doubt no one could touch Jackson because of the statute of limitations. Maybe the young rancher was safe. But maybe not. There had been several capital crimes, and what was still keeping the Dillin boys inside bars was the various species of manslaughter they committed, killing victims during the commission of a robbery.

Bates frowned. In that office, lawmen were probably pulling out old dodgers. Maybe preparing wires to lawmen in Montana and Wyoming. If they were writing letters, he intended to let Jackson know, postal regulations be damned. One thing they weren't doing—at least not yet: No one was rounding up Truman Jackson. They knew him as an honorable man, and they knew where they could find him.

Bates let himself into his post office, found a lucifer and lit the lamp. He wished he had cleaned the glass chimney because he wanted to read the old dodgers that accumulated at every post office in the country. But he would make do. He shuffled into his back room, pulled open a drawer, and withdrew a mighty stack of wanted sheets. They had been laid there by successive postmasters for years, so he dug deep. There, indeed, was one offering a $500 reward for information leading to the arrest of bank and train and stage robbers Rufe, Gin, and Monk Dillin, and Kid Dowd. Will wasn't even mentioned. He must have known that no one had even known there had been another, half-grown Dowd.

Bates sighed. This story was just beginning. He had always been fascinated by moral courage. It had come from his reading. He loved biography, and had examined the lives of great men, and sometimes great women, too. Most eminent men had not displayed moral character at all, but had risen by other means. But here and there were people Bates regarded as heroes. Especially American heroes, yeomen farmers, merchants, ordinary souls who had transcended the world. Now it looked like he had spotted another one. Someday, after he retired from the post office, he planned to write about them.

He surveyed his grubby office, which glimmered darkly in the lamplight, and lamented its grime. He always meant to be clean. Postal inspectors were forever rebuking him for his slovenly ways. And once in a long while he did burrow through the rubbish and undeliverable mail, throwing out a few items. But that didn't really interest him.

Courage did. Men fashioned of steel did. Souls reaching for the stars did. That was his real world, a world where brave men reached for perfection.

Someday he would write a book, or at least a chapter, about Truman Jackson. And about Cottonwood. And whether Jackson would remain there.

Chapter 7

The stupidity of criminals never failed to amuse Sheriff Styles Quail. He rode a good saddler toward the Jackson ranch, pondering the general ineptitude of lowlifes. He rather enjoyed a good crook, but not the dumb ones. They all had weaknesses he could exploit, but the brighter ones sometimes made a good chase out of it.

Truman Jackson was a case by himself. Of all the dumb things done by dumb people, Jackson's conduct was undoubtedly the dumbest. And proof yet again of the density of the criminal mind. Jackson's was obviously solid hickory, from ear to ear. Which was too bad because Jackson was a likable man.

When Quail first heard the amazing story from Henshaw, he could scarcely believe it. But there were witnesses enough to fill a dozen courtrooms. The man had publicly incriminated himself for crimes no one knew about.

Quail's first act had been to dig into musty files and extract ancient dodgers, notices, warrants, and requests from neighboring lawmen. A thorough search revealed absolutely nothing against Will Dowd, self-confessed bank, stage, and train robber. Indeed, the old descriptions of the Dillin-Dowd Gang did not even include the boy, who had somehow escaped the attention of lawmen in Montana and Wyoming.

That made Truman Jackson's sudden self-indictment all the more curious. Some men on the lam give up just for the relief of it. All that talk of taking a final step toward self-acceptance and restitution was all just talk and nothing more. But Quail wanted to hear it with his own ears, if only to marvel at the cunning of the outlaw brain.

He hadn't the faintest idea what would happen, but he aimed to contact lawmen wherever the gang had struck, and he didn't doubt that some extradition papers would land in Salt Lake for the governor's attention. Someday soon, some men wearing stars would stop at his office and show him some papers, and he would escort them out to the Jackson ranch. The old robberies could not be prosecuted because of the passage of time, but the several killings were another matter. And here was a self-confessed accomplice to those crimes.

The day was hotter than hell, and a rare humidity drew oily sweat out of Quail's face and soaked his armpits. He had escaped to the West as a boy because he couldn't stand the steamy summers back East; but this day reminded him of a June day in Baltimore.

Still, the open country solaced him, and the

steady rhythm of his good walking horse pleased him. He bore no warrants, but Quail wished he could haul this double-life fraud back to the courthouse and pen him until the county could unload him on some out-of-state deputy.

While he was at it, he was going to pin Gracie's ears back. If she had been in on any of the robberies, she would be heading for some women's wing somewhere. From what Henshaw told him, Gracie didn't look like she approved of any of Truman's little potluck-supper confession. Outlaw ladies were usually about twice as smart as outlaw men. Practical. A good moll didn't entertain crazy notions.

In spite of the humidity there hadn't been enough showers, and now the land lay brown and sere, although the Uintas rose darkly off to the north, promising water and forage for ranchers running out of graze. It was a good land, endowed with peace and quiet. Good people, too. Mostly Mormon, but plenty of Gentiles around, all living in harmony, all careful to abide by the laws of the land. Four churches in town: a Mormon temple, a Catholic, a Lutheran, and a combined Protestant. That's where Jackson stubbed his toe.

Quail wasn't any species of religionist himself, a fact he carefully concealed, especially around election time. Around then he got cozy with the Mormons, but never accepted their offers to sign him up. Nice people, who'd suffered plenty and built a paradise out of a harsh land.

He rode along the diminishing road, which ended at the Jackson ranch headquarters, climbing sharply the last mile or so, higher and higher above the tumbling south branch of the river below. He rounded a sharp bend and beheld the ranch glowing in the sun. Tidy, well cared for, peaceable. And run by a self-professed crook.

A pair of nondescript mutts announced his arrival, and he rode up to the veranda of the board-and-batten home, and dismounted, wrapping a rein around the hitch rail. By then Gracie had emerged.

"Gracie? Nice day, yeah? I need to talk to Truman."

She stared somberly, her gaze gliding over the bulky sheriff, observing the six-gun in its nest, the weathered face of a sixty-year-old man in the shade of a big sombrero, the gut hanging over his belt.

"Good afternoon, Sheriff."

"I heard about this potluck thing, and I just want a little visit with Truman."

"Are you going to arrest him?"

"Do I look like I've got a warrant?"

She didn't smile. "The barn loft. He's cleaning old hay out of it."

Quail saw Nell peering at him from the front door, and smiled. He liked kids, even the spawn of crooks. They weren't old enough to go bad yet.

"All right," he said. "I just gotta hear this."

Quail lumbered stiffly across a lawn ground down to dirt, to the barn, which was set lower on the soft slope. Two hours of riding made him stiff these days, and his pins weren't moving easily, protesting every step. Time to retire. But before he retired, he thought he'd just like to put one more crook behind bars.

He entered the cool darkness of the barn. Light filtered through numerous cracks in the walls, and a couple of small glassless windows. After the day's heat, the place felt good.

"Truman, you around here?"

He heard a rustling above, and Truman appeared at the edge of the half loft.

"Been expecting you, Mr. Quail," he said.

"Well, you mind coming down here and explaining what this is all about?"

Jackson nodded, set a pitchfork aside, and descended a ladder cobbled together of poles.

"You want to come up to the place for something to drink? Gracie's got some buttermilk. Maybe some lemonade."

"No, we'll just palaver right here. Henshaw was there last night, and I just want to hear whether he got his story right or whether he's as crazy as you."

Jackson looked sweaty as he walked by the big sliding doors, heading for the shady side of the barn and settling down with his back to the rough red planks.

"Little breeze here," he said. "Sure. I'll tell you just what I told the folks at the potluck."

And he did, in a quiet drone. It took scarcely five minutes.

"I just don't get this, Truman," the sheriff said. "Why'd you do this?"

"To make things right."

"I still don't get it."

"A man who's harmed others, and made his peace with God has a task remaining. Restitution. Best as I can, anyway."

Styles Quail shrugged that off. It didn't make sense. "Now, what I want is, who's chasing you? Someone must be closing in."

"No one."

"Well, let me put it this way. You got away clean. Why are you messing up your life?"

Jackson gazed at the horizon a moment. "It's just the opposite of messing up my life. It has more to do with putting it in order. A man should not be living a double life, surrounded by neighbors, friends, and merchants who trust him. He ought to find a way to open himself up to everyone. No false flags, just straight as one can be."

"That don't make much sense. You already had that. Now you don't."

He grinned slightly. "We'll see. Might lose some friends. Might gain some. I've spent years trying to grow. Gracie and me, we've studied on it. How do you get from where we started to what these good people are?"

"We? Was she in on it?"

"No, she worked for her ma, who ran a boardinghouse."

A smirk built on Quail's face. "Boardinghouse, eh?"

"You're thinking along lines that aren't true, Sheriff."

"Where was this boardinghouse, as you call it?"

"Fort Benton, Montana Territory."

"What was their name?"

"She had no father. Her mother's name was Fenway."

"No father!" Quail laughed.

Truman Jackson's face darkened. "I'm the only man Gracie ever had. I'll say it once and never talk about it again."

The tone prompted Quail to back off. You can't get much out of an angry man. He lifted a hand and gestured it away.

"Now, were you holding horses for the Dillin bunch and your uncle when they hit the Evanston bank?"

"Yes."

"Were you holding horses for the gang when they hit the stagecoach at Wolf Creek?"

"Yes."

"Were you holding them nags when they hit Thermopolis? And the Reed Point express car heist, when that express agent got himself shot through the neck?"

"Yes."

"Truman, you willing to write this stuff down?"

"Yes."

"I don't get why."

"So Gracie and I and the children can walk the earth as ourselves, at home with our Lord and our neighbors."

Quail shook his head. "It ain't gonna be like that, Truman. In every one of those cases you're confessing to, you were an accomplice to murder, and there's no statute of limitations on that."

"I know," he said.

Chapter 8

Weber Heeber ranched just below the Jacksons on the South Fork, and the Jacksons considered him their friend. Most people believed Weber Heeber was their friend, and he made sure that they always thought so.

What no one suspected about him was the extent of the bitterness that seethed and bubbled deep below his placid exterior. Least of all his wife, Pauline. He looked down his nose at her, but she hadn't the faintest idea that he did. She saw only his bland, good-humored mask, his opaque blue eyes that let no mortal peek within, and an inscrutable calm that never altered, even in difficult or joyous moments.

Heeber was perfectly aware of his masks, and delighted in them. There really was only one mask, that of a hale, middle-aged, shrewd rancher and businessman and politician, friend to all, and wise counselor in the affairs of Cottonwood.

He had discovered early in life that he considered Pauline beneath him. He disliked her bland food, served in mountainous heaps. He disliked her cow-like bellowing in moments of passion or joy or sadness, and he disliked about thirty other bad traits, such as her habit of effusing smiles and love upon him. He considered her a maudlin mother, spoiling the children with undisciplined emotion that gushed up like sewage. He thought she looked more like a heifer than a woman. He seethed when she spent money on herself. He knew she would never improve, and there was no point in educating, rebuking, or encouraging her.

She hadn't the faintest idea that she wasn't appreciated, and that's how he wanted it. He had always been secretive, but when she had entered his life, he had swiftly perfected his privacy, assuming a kindly, vague, attentive manner like that of a store clerk. She thought that was his nature, and in a sense she was right. That was his nature, but not all of it.

He was all things to all men. To the Jacksons, an amiable neighbor ready to help with roundups and haying. To the other county supervisors, he was a voice of quiet and moderation. To the State Bank of Cottonwood directors, he was a man of discretion and shrewdness. To people at Fourth of July gatherings and picnics and town meetings and the Grand Army of the Republic gatherings, he was the distant acquaintance, ever ready to pitch in.

They did not know him. Only Weber Heeber knew himself.

He had ranched at that site for two decades, always assuming that he could summer his stock high in the Uinta Mountains, and drive it down to lush, ungrazed pastures during colder times. He never dreamed that the Jacksons would arrive and homestead above him on land he considered his own, land he had used and felt he had a right to.

But there they were. With industry and aggressiveness, Truman Jackson had swiftly expanded the place, proving up land and buying more, driving his stock high into the mountains, just as Weber Heeber had done. That rankled him so much that sometimes Heeber spent hours devising ways of ruining the Jacksons. He was, after all, a county supervisor, owner of the bank, and one of the most influential businessmen in town, with a half interest in the feed store and livery barn. But every time he thought of it, he was deterred by prudence. The Jacksons had rooted down and become very popular.

Gracie Jackson was forever driving over with a fresh pie for the Heebers. Truman usually had timothy hay to spare, and offered it to Weber at generous rates, rates that would make his livery stable and feed store more profitable. So Heeber had always bought, thanked Jackson for his generous terms, and kept his seething anger well hidden from sight.

This trait, which he had honed to perfection, he considered a great virtue. With it, he had maintained perfect domestic harmony. With it, he had avoided making enemies and had become something of a politician. Because of it, he was widely esteemed, considered a sober and judicious man whose views were well weighed and measured.

With it, he could utterly conceal darker feelings—anger, bitterness, or even frivolity—from a nosy and gossipy town.

Heeber did not hear about the potluck confession, as it was being called around Cottonwood, for two days because he had been busy on his ranch. But when he did finally take the spring wagon to town to pick up some stock salt and a few groceries, he heard the whole story swiftly enough. First from one of the county supervisors, Rafael Dinwiddy, and then from the president of the bank, Elton James, then from Andy Blitz, who operated the feed store and elevator, and finally from his friend Red Bork right on the street. The stories mostly matched. Jackson had once been an outlaw with a notorious and deadly gang. A boy, yes, but at the age of discretion, the age when anyone knew right and wrong.

"And why this now?" Weber asked.

"That's being argued. Mostly because he felt like it," Cowper said.

"People don't do that because they feel like it."

Cowper scoffed. "Well, Jackson said it was to make himself whole and practice his faith, but you and I know how religion's used to veneer realities. I reckon he just got tired of runnin'."

Heeber smiled, or allowed himself the slight lightening of his serious nature that people took for amiability. Then he headed for the Zion Restaurant and ordered himself a piece of quince pie and a glass of milk, and began to think on the extraordinary news. The damn fool had thrown it all away.

After refreshing himself, he strolled back to the courthouse for a visit with Styles Quail, and discovered that Quail was already hard at work on the matter. There was not a single dodger or warrant in the files for Will Dowd, but that wasn't slowing Quail down. He'd interviewed Jackson and heard the story himself, written and wired lawmen across two states for more information, and was awaiting word.

Heeber smiled blandly.

"Good work, Styles" was all he said, and returned to the summer heat.

There would be hell to pay. Sooner or later some aggressive county attorney was going to go after Jackson, stage a showy trial with all sorts of hair-raising evidence, and put the man away for twenty years.

So Jackson wished to abandon his double life, cleanse himself, and step into Cottonwood a reformed man. That was understandable. Also a fool's mission. Jackson didn't need to do that; he was a trusted and model citizen and had been so for years. But he did it. And that would be Heeber's opportunity.

The world progressed in mysterious ways, and now Weber Heeber was going to acquire the pasture, much improved and fenced, that had been snatched from him a dozen years earlier. And for pennies on the dollar. If need be, Heeber would nudge matters along. A word from a county supervisor to the sheriff carried weight. A word to a merchant, a word to his feed store staff, a word to neighbors. A word to his wife. Nothing more than a thought quietly implanted by a quiet man. But they would all take seed, and Heeber would have improved land for ten percent of its value.

He did not pity the Jacksons. They had arrived in Cottonwood flying false colors, and deserved whatever the law would mete out to them. Jackson had conveniently waited for the statutes of limitation to run out before having his attack of conscience. If the man had pronounced himself a stagecoach bandit a year or so after arriving, when he was still liable, that would have been impressive. But all crooks calculate, and no doubt Jackson had kept an eye on his calenders. If Gracie had been in on it, she deserved her fate as well.

For a moment he was troubled by his own harshness. But it passed. He was of the school that said there could be no true reform, even when someone wanted it. Once a crook, always a crook. Once a murderer, always a murderer. Once a woman of dubious reputation, never a lady. Gracie was obviously a scarlet woman; who else would run with a train robber? People only pretended to reform themselves. That ran against theology, but it was common sense. One didn't see reformed criminals because there weren't any.

That pleasant afternoon in sunbaked Cottonwood, he arranged for a line of credit at his bank. That would take care of the land. He didn't want Jackson's livestock.

Then he headed for his feed store and instructed Andy Blitz to deny Jackson credit.

"Cash on the barrelhead, Andy."

"Because of the confession?"

"Well, if his bank assets turn out to be stolen, they'll be frozen by the county attorney," he said patiently. "And we need to be paid."

"You think he should go to the pen?"

"If he's found guilty, of course."

"All his good time here don't count?"

"Everything counts. Maybe there should be a light sentence. But no one in his right mind would ever trust Jackson."

"Yeah, I get the point," Blitz said.

"Mind you, I have nothing against the man. He's been a good neighbor."

"Well, you can't be too careful. I always knew there was something wrong with Jackson," Blitz said. "I could just feel it."

Heeber counted it a good afternoon. He rode quietly back to his ranch, raising powdery dust from the wheels of his spring wagon, and thinking long thoughts about virtue and vice.

He faced another task, which was to persuade his wife that the Jacksons weren't to be trusted. But that would be easy. Pauline would lap up every bit of wisdom he served to her. The secret lay in his blandness.

He drove into his place, sweltering in the oppressive late afternoon heat, and found her resting on the porch, in the wicker rocker.

"Too hot, Weber. Too hot," she said.

"Yep, like the hinges of hell," he said. "I reckon that's where Truman and Gracie are headed . . ."

Chapter 9

The next days seemed peaceable enough to Truman Jackson. Except for the sheriff's visit, he suffered no reaction to his revelation. But he was not fooled. There would be trouble, and he sometimes wondered whether Cottonwood would let him rehabilitate himself.

Gracie withdrew into her own world. The boys helped with the fencing. It would be two months before school and the taunts of other children, and Jackson hoped that by then the whole thing would die away.

He pondered the possibility of old cases being reopened. He thought it was possible, but he also believed that a dozen or so years of life as a good citizen would be enough to temper the ambitions of prosecutors. He knew he had friends in Cottonwood, no matter what had been revealed, and he was not alone.

That Sunday he took his family to church. He couldn't attend every Sunday because of the great distance to town, but the Jacksons never went long without filling a pew. This particular Sunday he would attend with his whole family. It was important. He wanted the congregation to see them together, just as they were before the potluck supper: together, loving, being the sort of citizens that Cottonwood cherished.

So he loaded them into the buckboard, and they drove the long dusty road to town. As they neared Cottonwood, he cautioned them.

"Now, there'll be some people who won't know what to do or say because I told 'em I'd done some bad things when I was a boy. Just smile and be friendly. I don't think they'll judge us. If they do, just ignore 'em. We're coming to worship God in His house, and we'll be just fine."

He wasn't so sure of that.

He dropped his family at the front of the white clapboard church, ignoring the stares, and drove his rig off to a shady area where the majestic cottonwoods arched over the horses and rig, and then walked back to the church.

He knew at once, as he ascended the steps to the lobby, that things were going to be hard. Some people greeted him with an abrupt nod, others turned away. The ushers escorted the Jacksons to their usual pew, but this time no one sat beside them. He and Gracie and Jon and Parker and Nell sat in terrible isolation, while around them the congregation hulked in dour silence.

He sighed. He had done what he had to do. He had taken one last step to complete his transformation from a youthful outlaw to a good citizen. He could only wait and see. Where were his old friends? Where were those who had invited the Jacksons to their table?

Then things began. Heather Hjortsbergen played the processional on the pump organ, the choir and the Reverend Eli Pickrell took their places, and the service proceeded as it always did, through the lessons and hymns. The collection plate made its rounds, and was followed by the doxology.

Then it was time for the sermon. Mr. Pickrell arose, settled himself behind the pulpit, and surveyed his congregation.

"I am very glad the Jacksons are here today," he said. "I am going to talk about events in this church."

Truman worried that he was about to be rebuked, and slid his fingers into Gracie's tense hand.

"Actually, I'm going to talk about repentance, growth, and acceptance of every soul who comes to God."

That sounded hopeful. A small, amiable smile from Pickrell in the direction of the Jacksons heartened Truman.

"This is a great time for our church," Pickrell said. "For there is no greater joy in heaven or on earth when the lost are found, and the strayed are welcomed into our fold."

That pleased Jackson. He had a true friend and ally in Eli Pickrell.

"I can point to numerous texts in the Scriptures in which the Lord welcomed a repenting sinner; times when He rebuked those who wanted to exclude those who had sinned and repented and sought a way home. Yes, this week has been the most beautiful and triumphant in the brief history of this church, and in my own ministry . . ."

Pickrell was delivering a heartfelt welcome to Truman Jackson, and he wanted every soul in his congregation to know it. He talked of sorrow, growth, the promptings of conscience, and finally about Truman Jackson's long path toward goodness and godliness, topped now not only by a public acknowledgment of his youthful ways, but also by a desire to make amends.

Eli Pickrell was giving more than a sermon: he was insisting that his congregation welcome Jackson, nurture him in his new life, help him complete the restitution that he had announced as his personal goal. And above all, make him welcome and cherished, for that was what churches are for.

Jackson peered about unobtrusively. Some were rapt; some sat in stony silence.

Then a terrible thing happened: Mrs. Sitgreaves arose, gathered her parasol, worked her way to the center aisle, and left.

Eli Pickrell paused while the congregation watched.

"I've said enough. You know how I stand. How this congregation must stand if it calls itself Christian. It is time for prayer and the searching of our hearts."

He led them at once in a swift, piercing prayer, asking God to soften hard hearts, to bless Truman

Jackson and comfort his family, and for his flock to welcome the Jacksons every day, evermore, Amen.

In five minutes it was over.

People filed out, most of them shaking hands with Mr. Pickrell at the door. Truman watched a dozen slip out the rear door. Bob Scott came up and shook Truman's hand. So did Bill Howell. And so did Hamlin Henshaw, deputy sheriff, and his wife, which surprised Jackson. Minerva Constance Welsh didn't shake hands with Truman, but grasped Gracie's. Rafael Dinwiddy, county supervisor, smiled briefly from across the sanctuary, but kept his hand unsullied.

The Jacksons were almost the last to leave. Truman didn't want to embarrass anyone in line, so they waited.

But at last, on the brink of sunlight, Jackson reached Pickrell.

"Thank you," he said, not knowing what else to say.

"We should be thanking you, Truman. You've shown us the way and given us a lesson."

"Well, I just did what I had to."

"Please come back to my office," the minister said. "Bring the children or not, as you choose."

So there was trouble. Jackson nodded.

A few minutes later, in a small ell off the sanctuary, Pickrell hung up his robes and settled behind a plain desk while Jackson and Gracie stood waiting.

"There are things you should know," Pickrell said. "The first and most important is that Thursday night, following the potluck, a delegation of ten visited me at the parsonage. I'm not going to tell you who they are, or sow more seeds of division. They claimed to be speaking for a large majority. I doubt it. I think just now most of our people are fence-sitting. They haven't come to any conclusions. Anyway, they had a very simple message: they were planning to expel you from the membership of this congregation, and they wanted my support. But if I didn't give it, they were going to do it anyway. They were going to call a special meeting to do it. And they weren't going to invite you, either. They wanted to be able to discuss it freely, without you around, they said. Then they were going to poll the entire membership."

Jackson nodded. "I feared it."

"I argued that anyone doing that was behaving in a most un-Christian manner, and that I would resist with every fiber of my being. The church draws people to it who need God; it doesn't expel them.

"Well, you can guess the arguments. I won't go into them. A blot on the membership, all that. And you know what I said? 'Friends, you had better expel me first, because I will not permit a congregation to defy the very teachings of Jesus Christ.' That set 'em back some. Their minister saying they'd better kick him out first, if they're going to give you the boot.

"That was good. I saw one or two of that delegation start to falter a little. Suddenly they weren't so sure. After all this talk about respectability and keeping the congregation free of evil, all of a sudden some of them blinked. But most of them just laid out a disgusting line. They want to put up walls so high no one could ever be a member of this church. And I'm for tearing down walls and telling people the Gospel.

"Well . . . we were all talking softly and people were being brotherly, if that's what you call it, but talking brotherly soft was just about the same as brotherly shouting. And when they did finally file out of my home, I thought I'd been in a yelling match.

"I don't have much to say except if you go, I'll likely go. And I am your friend and admirer. I believe you're one of those called to be with God. And I'm going to wade into Cottonwood and defend you in the streets and on the rooftops and in the fields and the kitchens, wherever I can find someone who'll listen."

"Mr. Pickrell . . ." Truman wanted to say that the minister shouldn't sacrifice himself or his pastoral life just for one old stagecoach bandit. But it didn't come out that way.

". . . thank you."

"Well, don't thank me. Thank the good Lord for giving you a new life. Now, you go back out there in peace. And I'll confide in you that you've a few fine friends. Some people don't like this effort to push you out. For the moment, I won't say who your friends are, either. Dust needs to settle. But you're not alone, Truman. Not alone by a long shot, and there's plenty in Cottonwood who admire every step you've taken. I'll name just one: Father Mcgivern at St. Mary's. He stopped by to tell me. There are more, Truman and Gracie. So take heart."

They drove back to the ranch filled with joy and foreboding.

Chapter 10

Truman Jackson unbolted a plank in the old wagon that had seen them through the long exodus from Montana to Utah, and extracted a small oilcloth-wrapped packet from its secret hollow in the wagon, and then bolted the plank back in place.

That evening he lit a kerosene lamp, placed it on the battered kitchen table, and unwrapped the packet. Within were a dozen yellowed clippings.

"Jackson, do you really want to do this?" Gracie asked. "We have so many needs. The mortgage . . . the children require new clothing for school . . ."

"This is the most important need," he said.

Gracie nodded. She worried more than he did that the troubles in town would escalate. He thought they would just wither away. A dozen years of good citizenship wouldn't be washed away just by a confession of youthful crime, he believed.

She sat beside him as he unfolded the clippings, one by one. Each told the tale of a robbery by the Dillin-Dowd gang. They read the old clippings with sadness, if not torment. People shot. People losing their life's savings. A bride who lost her wedding ring and twenty-nine dollars. A mother who lost every cent she was carrying to a daughter who had lost a husband and needed money to start a boardinghouse. A mine payroll. The mine had collapsed, being unable to pay its help.

But most of the victims were simply people who were relieved of whatever was in their pockets, and the gang walked through railroad cars, lined up people on stagecoaches, emptied the pockets of customers in banks.

Upon examining each clipping, Truman wrote the names of the victims on a sheet of foolscap, and if the victim's hometown or destination was listed, he wrote that down, too. There were many Montana and Wyoming addresses: Fort Shaw, Helena, Fort Benton, Carroll, Virginia City, Three Forks, Cheyenne, Laramie, Rock Springs . . .

The more he read, the more disheartened he was. The victims were sketchily identified. He scarcely knew how to begin the process of restitution. Still, there were half a dozen he could start with.

"If we reach all of them, it'd cost us three hundred forty-seven dollars," he said.

"No, Truman. You were one of six. We owe them one-sixth of that. Around sixty dollars."

He grinned and shook his head. "When you're trying to make people whole, one-sixth doesn't do."

"But we can't—"

"We'll do what we can."

"Well, we won't even find most of them. That's a blessing."

"I wish we could find every last one."

She stared at him with a gaze he knew reflected both fear and love. She loved his courage, even if she worried herself sick about what might come.

He experienced no pain until he began to pen the letters. He was never much with the English language, and writing a coherent letter was worse than a month in jail. But he had to do it. He would scratch out his letters and hope they would wing their way to people who might have moved half a dozen times in the following twelve or fifteen years.

"Dear Mr. Shumann," he wrote. "On May 14, 1869, you were robbed of a silver pocket watch, a ring, and forty-three dollars in cash near Helena, Montana.

"I was one of those in the gang that held up the stagecoach. I wish to make amends. If you will put a value on the watch and ring, I will send you a bank draft for that amount and the cash you lost.

"Sincerely . . ."

He blotted the letter and folded it into an envelope and addressed it: Henry Shumann, Clancy, Montana Territory. In the upper corner he penned his name and Cottonwood, Utah.

" Well, Gracie, that's number one."

She nodded somberly. "I'm afraid. But I'm glad, too. Oh, Truman . . ."

He reached across the table and touched her

hand. She looked so lovely in that warm lamplight.
She had stood by him the whole distance, from
Montana to Utah, from boy bandit to respected
rancher, from angry cynic to a man who had accepted his Lord.

She smiled.

He penned several more letters, sometimes
scratching out words, sometimes crumpling the
paper and pitching it aside. Writing a letter was
sweaty work, and he loathed it. He had not got beyond eighth grade, and didn't know half the words
that more educated men used. But he knew his
way of communicating was direct and blunt, and
that those letters would tell the story.

But when he was done, and tried to scrub ink
stains from his fingers, he knew he had scarcely
begun a task that would consume him.

He scanned the clippings again, recording names
that were not connected to any city, surnames without a first name: Mr. Smith, Mrs. Jones. There were
over eighty of those. And he recorded the names of
the companies and firms that had been hurt as
well. It made a sad and dark list. The gang had
hurt so many, robbed people of dreams and hopes.
And killed several.

He reflected on his origins, the son of an outlaw,
the son of a tormented woman living in a remote
ranch where the gang kept its horses. His mother
had been at once loving and tender toward him,
but suspicious and angry at the world, blaming
bankers, capitalists, storekeepers, stupid doctors,

crooked neighbors for her misfortunes. Blaming everything and everyone—except herself.

Jackson reflected soberly that he had believed those things himself, had the same cast of mind inherited from his parents, and had barely escaped that fantasy world populated by vicious people into a kinder world. Somehow, along the way, he had learned not to ask what he could get away with, but to ask himself what was right. Once he had learned to ask the right question before he acted, the world was transformed. Somehow, things became all right.

The next morning he threw his old stock saddle over the bay gelding and headed for town. The ranch would take care of itself on a hot summer's day. The boys would be out checking the herd. Nell would be helping her mother.

He reached Cottonwood mid-morning, and tied up before the post office. He was ahead of the mail, and wanted to talk to Horatio Bates a moment.

He discovered the flabby old postmaster smoking a pipe behind the counter. Sweet tobacco smoke curled toward a window clouded with a year's accumulation of grime.

"Got a moment, Horatio?"

"Ah, the prodigal son. Sure, come and share my spittoon."

"Well, I'd prefer to share your wisdom," Jackson said, easing into a grubby wooden swivel chair.

Briefly Jackson described the next step in his effort to undo his past. "So I'm trying to locate these people. Trouble is, twelve, fifteen, sixteen years have gone by, and I don't have addresses. These here"—he waved his half-dozen letters—"are addressed poorly, just a name and a town. You think they'll get there?"

"A few. Truman, this is just the most outstanding thing I've ever seen. Doing this, trying to find these people the gang robbed."

"It's just another step along the road for me, Horatio. Once you get going on this road, you've got to go to the end of it."

"But, Truman, you just held horses. You can't take all this on your shoulders."

"That's what Gracie said, but I figure we were all in it together. If I hadn't held the horses, we wouldn't have gotten away so good. The rest are dead or in the pen, so I'm the one has to put things right."

"You're going too far with it, Truman."

"Horatio, I'm doing what I have to do. Now, can you help me? I've got a list here of people, some just surnames, and I don't know where they're from. Like this Mrs. Barnes from New York and that Mr. Noble. There's a Mrs. Border in White Sulphur Springs, but no first name."

"You really want to contact all those people? There's risk in it."

"No path is without risk, Horatio."

The postmaster donned his spectacles and surveyed the list.

"Few here I can try. I'll write to the postmasters where there's a place mentioned. Ask 'em about these people. But that was long ago and you're going to run into dead ends, mostly. But I'll do what I can, Truman. Isn't hardly a man in the whole United States that'd do what you're trying to do."

"Gracie thinks I'm stretching it. We don't know if we can pay for a tenth of what's owed back. And I'm not even talking about interest. But we're going to go the whole distance, Horatio."

"You don't need to. Most people think mighty kindly of you just for coming forward. No one expects you to repay. You were a kid, Truman. You hadn't even reached your majority."

"I knew we were doing wrong."

"But you were born to it. The outlaw family. Famous in a dozen states, the Dowds. You ought to let up on yourself."

"Well, just help me find these people. I'll pay your postage."

"You'd have to. I can't just send letters out."

"Here's a cartwheel, Horatio. When you use it up, let me know and I'll keep you in stamps."

"This is just so fine I'll be proud to do it. I've never seen the like, Truman."

"Well, I'll stay in town until you put the mail up. I'm going to go over and talk to the sheriff."

"He want you?"

"No, I'm going to ask him to get me every indictment against the gang. Then I'll have names and addresses and amounts taken and what's what."

Bates puffed a moment, contemplating that. "He

may not arrest you, Truman, because he's got nothing on you here. But don't count him a friend."

Jackson stood. "It's in me to make every man a friend," he said. "Even Styles Quail, though it's a problem."

Chapter 11

Jackson tracked the sheriff to the Boscobel, a grubby eatery around the corner from the courthouse. The sheriff was wolfing mashed potatoes covered with stringy brown gravy, and a heap of gray beef.

"What?" Quail asked.

"I need to talk to you."

Quail motioned toward the opposing seat with his fork. "You want to turn yourself in?"

Jackson sat quietly and let the sheriff chow down a moment.

"I'm wanting to begin repaying people. I think I can do that, if the ranch keeps going and I don't get grasshoppered out or something like that."

"Repay people? What are you talking about?"

"The gang. They robbed people. I was part of it. I owe some people some money."

"What you owe is a life in the pen."

Jackson ignored that. "I owe people some money, and I want your help finding them."

The sheriff looked nonplussed. "Help? Finding them?"

"Yes. Get me the complaints that put my cousins away. Get me the indictments from Montana and Wyoming. Then I can start tracking people down."

"Are you even crazier than I thought? First you confess to crimes no one suspected. Accessory to some killings, it seems. Now you want to fork over money. I don't get it. Are you suicidal or what?"

Jackson spoke slowly and carefully. "I want to set my life right, both for my own sake and the people who suffered. I want to recompense people who were hurt. I want to stand before God and tell him I've done all I could to make myself acceptable to him. I want to be accepted by my neighbors who know how I started life . . . and what I am now. Open book. No secrets. To win forgiveness there has to be repentance. To win a new life, I have to pay old debts. Does that make sense?"

"No. What you owe is ten years in the pen on each count. You commit a crime, and you owe the government a fine and a sentence."

"Not the victims?"

"You should have thought about the victims before you held horses for your gang."

"That's not what I asked, Styles."

"Now it's Styles, is it? Stagecoach robber calls the sheriff by his first name. First you confess to capital crimes, then you get second thoughts and try to butter everyone up by spreading a few cartwheels in the direction of a few of your victims. Get you off the hook. But it ain't the victims you owe, Jackson."

That line of reasoning puzzled Jackson. Did the

sheriff really believe that when a wrong was done, the offense was done only against the law and the government? But he saw no point in arguing it. The man had his own way of thinking.

"Just get me copies of the indictments so I can find out the names of people. I've written a few."

Quail lifted a fork. "Written a few? So they can file a civil suit against you? Where do you hide your brains, Jackson? I swear, crooks are the dumbest breed alive. Born dumb. It's in the blood. Dumb enough to commit crimes, stupid enough to wreck their lives. You can't ever escape it. I never heard of a crook going straight for long. Year or two, maybe. But not for long. Maybe the upbringing. I don't care what it is, only that they always go haywire. You gonna dispute it? I got fourteen years of experience in law enforcement proving it."

"I guess I'll be going," Jackson said, standing up. He realized that half the people in the restaurant had been eavesdropping. As he stood, people swiftly averted their eyes.

"Jackson, I've already written every damned lawman in both those states. They'll extradite you just as fast as they can manage it. You'll learn soon enough who you murdered, but you'll be behind bars instead of shelling out a few hundred dollars."

Jackson nodded.

"And don't you leave this county, or I'll come after you."

"I am a free man, sheriff. There is no bill against me here. Or anywhere."

"Not anymore you ain't."

That rankled Jackson, but he held his peace and slipped through the greasy spoon and into the sunlight. It felt good to be outdoors.

Funny, he thought, the things you learn about people. For Sheriff Quail, crime was a matter between a lawbreaker and the government, like a pair of gladiators in an arena. A man who had wronged others could repay his victims fourfold, make everything right, and it wouldn't matter to Quail.

He stood in the dust of the street, wondering what his fate might be. His dream lay shattered, and now he was in grave trouble. His family was, too, and might soon be broken and impoverished. What had he done to Gracie and the children? No wonder she had dreaded the whole thing, and begged him not to reveal himself. She had understood the perversity of the human beast far better than he.

And yet . . . he was not ashamed of his choice. Now he would not have to live a double life, being Truman Jackson to his neighbors but still Will Dowd deep within. Now he was a step closer to being the Christian he wanted to be. Now he had set in motion a plan to make the gang's victims whole . . . at least as far as his means could do that. He scarcely knew how he would repay a mine company payroll, but he knew one thing: whatever burden he had placed upon himself, it was a burden that would please his Lord and God. He hoped it would please others, too.

Cottonwood lifted his spirits. Before him was the square, guarded by majestic cottonwood trees that cast sun-dappled shade over the dusty park, which sheltered old-timers who sat on benches and whittled wood and told tales. A few children swirled like flocking birds, and a woman pushed a perambulator toward an empty bench and sat, fanning herself.

Beyond, the broad artery of Cottonwood, Utah Avenue, divided the town. The city fathers had planted cottonwoods along it, and now these swift-growing trees arched over the street and shaded the shops on either side, making the town comfortable even on a sweltering day.

He loved this place and felt at home in it. He had been here for all of his adult life. Growing up, he had thought of home as a hideout, a refuge from a vicious world, secretive, guarded by mountain walls, but with an exit trail for quick escapes. That was what he had called home. A den against the whole world. Now, as he gazed upon this gracious young town, he knew that home was infinitely more. It was neighbors and butchers and bakers and churches. It was knowing everyone and being known. It was being trusted—and trusting others. Trusting the bank not to steal his money. Trusting the butcher not to put his thumb on the scale. Trusting in the safety of the place. Trusting that his children could grow up here, secure and happy and enjoying friends. He knew, at last, the meaning of that puzzling word, "hometown." Cottonwood was his hometown.

He figured he knew about half of Cottonwood personally, and most of the rest by name. He saw people at peace, walking the serene boulevard, unhurried, unafraid. Gracie loved this place, too, and the children loved it as well. They saw Cottonwood through the lens of the ice-cream parlor, where Truman sometimes treated them to a delicious dish of vanilla, or a phosphate.

Now, at last, he had shed his mask and invited Cottonwood to accept him for what he was: a man with a dark past, but a mortal who for a dozen years had been a good citizen, helping and building this place.

He had a few more errands, and then he would ride out to the ranch. Tomorrow would begin the haying—grueling toil but one that would give him a pile of prairie hay to feed his horses through the winter. The cattle always had to fend for themselves, but the winters were usually mild, and his losses were few, except when the occasional storm hit.

He headed for the State Bank of Cottonwood, which had been erected from the same red sandstone as the courthouse. It occupied the corner of Utah and Second, lording over the town with amiable confidence.

He entered its cool confines and found the young cashier, Bob Scott, at the teller's wicket.

"I'd like to withdraw twenty dollars, Bob," he said.

"Ah, Jackson, can't do that."

"What's the trouble?"

"Well, we can't let you have money from your

account. Can't let you debit it, either. It's sort of complex."

"It's my money! You have no right—"

"Look, go talk to Elton James. He'll explain it."

"Does this have anything to do with the potluck supper?"

"You go back there and Elton'll explain it."

Jackson stormed toward the president's alcove and loomed over the balding man.

"What's the trouble here? I want my money!"

"Oh, sit down, Jackson. No problem. It seems there's been some question about your accounts, is all."

Jackson eased himself tautly into the chair, across the marble-topped desk from the bank's executive. "There is no problem with my accounts, Elton."

"Well, yes. Some people are whispering that maybe your funds are . . . well, suspect. A bank can't harbor ill-gotten funds, you know. Against the law."

"I've been here twelve years, ranching and doing my best. You know that."

"Well, not everyone does know that. Seems you've been suspected for a long time of certain . . . practices."

"Who? What?"

"Well, Weber Heeber dropped by, owner and chairman of the board you know, and asked me to put a hold on your accounts. We can do that. All demand accounts are actually thirty-day demand. We don't have to pay out anything for thirty days if we have reason not to, and he says that'll be time enough."

"Enough for what?"

"Well, he said, he's going out to look at your stock. Taking Arch Understreet along. Livestock detective, that sort of thing." Elton James smiled. "Just thirty days, Jackson. If all's well, we'll be happy to debit your account. I'll make a note of it."

Moments later Truman Jackson stepped onto Utah Avenue, and Cottonwood no longer seemed so much like home.

Chapter 12

Jackson settled the bay into a mile-eating jog. He wanted to deal with Weber Heeber just as fast as possible. If Heeber was suspicious, as he had every right to be, Jackson wanted to show him every receipt he had, every branding record, everything that would settle his neighbor's doubts.

He and Gracie had done it the hard way, but the only way. They had each homesteaded a half section above Heeber's place, land that other ranchers had scorned because it was too steep, the South Fork running too far down in a canyon.

He and Gracie had worked ceaselessly, often for Weber and Pauline Heeber. They had bought bummed calves for a dollar, picked up crippled cattle no one wanted, added to the herd from their earnings. Many of his cattle had descended from the shorthorn bums they had bought from Heeber, giving the herd a distinctive red color. He wished now he had gotten a bill of sale for every bum he had bought from his neighbor. But they had been friendly, and it hardly seemed necessary. Time and time again, Heeber had said, "You want a bum calf? If you don't, I'll knock it in the head."

Bum calves were a lot of work, a lot of hand-feeding, and few ranchers tried to save them. Gracie had worked, too, often helping Pauline Heeber preserve her fruits and vegetables, earning a little here and there, even while raising their own children. There were no receipts; these had been neighborly arrangements. And now they boded trouble for the Jacksons.

Truman was not a naive man. He knew that Heeber hadn't liked it when the Jacksons homesteaded above them, effectively blocking passage up the creek to summer pasture in the Uintas. He knew that Heeber coveted the place now that the Jacksons had shown it was good ranching country. Over the years the Jacksons had bought more proved-up land from failed homesteaders, and now had four sections and a herd of three hundred, many of them descendants of bummed calves and cripples that couldn't be moved from pasture to pasture.

Up until the potluck revelation, Heeber had been a good neighbor, courteous and even generous. But somehow, everything had changed, and Jackson sensed that his biggest trouble would come not from the law, but from his own neighbor and friend. Heeber was on the move.

This summoning of Arch Understreet worried Jackson. Understreet was one of a half dozen range detectives employed by the Utah Stock Growers Association to curb rustling. They were empowered to inspect brands and arbitrate disputes. Understreet was young and stuffy and a little proddy, but otherwise amiable enough. He knew cattle, was loyal to the association, and usually arrived at a fair decision when it came to disputed stock. But he seemed to swagger a little, daring anyone to complain. Jackson never protested, not even when both decisions went against him on the two occasions Understreet decided the ownership of a slick calf.

Now Understreet would be looking at him from a new perspective, and that meant big trouble. The association had teeth. Even though it was a private group, it could make or break any ranch in Utah. It maintained a blacklist, and if any rancher were so unfortunate as to end up on that list, it meant the railroads wouldn't ship his stock, and most meat packers or butchers wouldn't buy it, either. Furthermore, most cattlemen wouldn't sell stock to a blacklisted rancher.

The ways a rancher ended up on the list remained mysterious. The decision was always made at a closeted meeting of the executive board of the association, and Jackson knew that hard proof—blotched brands, and other signs of theft—wasn't always necessary. Suspicion was all that counted, and if the suspicion fell upon a small rancher next to a powerful one, all the worse for the small rancher. Like Truman Jackson. Heeber was a board member of the Stock Growers Association as well as county supervisor, bank director, and pioneer landholder. And now that Jackson had revealed an outlaw past, he didn't doubt that Heeber's own covetousness had burgeoned in his chest. Jackson had always intuited that side of Weber Heeber.

Jackson hurried the bay along through a hot afternoon, and when the Heeber ranch road struck off to the left, Jackson turned down it, past familiar brown pastures, copses of cottonwoods, lazy red cattle chewing their cud, a windmill, a fenced-off hay field, and finally the white clapboard ranch house. The place sang of beauty and comfort and a settled, solid way of life spread over the best bottoms and foothills in the whole county.

He was in luck. As he jogged the bay into the Heeber ranch yard, he discovered Weber and Arch Understreet saddling up beside the weathered barn.

They looked startled as he rode up.

"I'm glad I caught you," Jackson said, noting the sudden masks that locked in place upon the faces of both men. "I'm just coming back from town, and Elton James told me you're entertaining some doubts about my herd. That's natural, and I understand it. A man who tells the world he was an outlaw when he was a kid isn't going to be trusted, at least not for a while."

Understreet was grinning wolfishly, having heard, with his own ears, what everyone was whispering about. But Heeber just squinted coldly. "The association's going to have a look."

"You're welcome to examine every animal on my ranch, including the horses. And I'll invite you into our house and show you every receipt and bill of sale I have. And I'll go a step farther. If you're positive in your mind that one or another animal is yours, some calf or heifer or whatever, you just let me know, and take it with you. Give me a receipt for it. Good neighbors don't argue about that. I'll trust you to do what's right, and hope you'll trust me."

He spoke firmly, amiably, but with a certain brusque passion, and noted the faint surprise in the faces of both men.

"It's not a cow or two I'm worried about. It's the whole herd. How'd you get it? You came here penniless."

"You know the answer to that. Bums that you gave me or I bought for a dollar. Heifers I took in payment for working for you, haying, fencing, building pens. The nickels and dimes Gracie earned here, with Pauline and all up and down the road, cleaning, preserving, weeding, and all the rest. Hard work, Weber."

"That stuff wouldn't keep a family in food, much less let you buy cattle," Understreet said.

Jackson sighed. It had come to this, then. He knew as well as these two did where this road would end. "Branding's about to begin. Why don't you come back then and look at the slick calves and how they're paired up. Everyone always has reps at every ranch anyway. That should settle the matter."

"It settles nothing, Jackson," Arch said ominously.

Jackson sat his bay quietly. "You are honorable men, answering to your conscience and to God.

Whatever you do will be done before the eyes of God. Whatever I did as a boy, and whatever I do now, has been before the throne of God and his judgment. Go have a look, then. You'll see a lot of shorthorn blood in the herd, and the foundation was the bum calves I bought or was given by you, Weber."

"I don't recollect more than one or two."

"Shall we go ask Pauline?"

That so startled Heeber that he swore, something that Jackson had never heard before from his lips. "You keep her out of this!"

Jackson turned to Understreet. "Be sure to ask her how many bums I bought or was given."

Understreet laughed derisively. "Women exaggerate," he said.

"Go look at my herd, then. I'll go with you if you wish."

"We don't."

"I'll have the records and receipts for you at the ranch house."

"Paper is mostly written-down lies."

"It's my wish to live peaceably with my friends and neighbors. It's also my desire that they be neighbors, and do what is right to me. I've treated you as you would want to be treated, and now I'm asking that you treat me as you would want to be treated. That's the law given us by someone a lot more important than ourselves."

He was making them uncomfortable. They were obviously expecting threats and anger and rage;

they received a small reminder of what it meant to be just.

Truman was shaking. He had wanted to yell at them, threaten them, take the fight to them. But he hadn't. This had been the hardest test in his new-found life, and he had passed it.

He rode up the ranch road while they finished saddling, and cut across pastures. He had surprised them with a weapon they hadn't considered: the sting of conscience. They might delude themselves that they were doing the right thing, but still, a small voice would whisper to them in the nights, and that voice had more authority than any brace of six-guns. It was odd, a former outlaw reminding Cottonwood's leading and most esteemed citizen of the Golden Rule, and maybe the First Commandment as well.

Yet he felt melancholic. He feared that he was about to lose the herd and the ranch he and Gracie had struggled so hard to build up.

He paused, reining in the bay slightly, to enjoy the serenity of the afternoon. The good land glowed. The grasses, rich and rain-blessed, carpeted the hills. A playful breeze caught his hair and drew the faint sheen of sweat off him. This was a good land, and he intended to stay. He would fight for his land, his good name, his herd, his newborn reputation. He would begin by telling everyone he met of this encounter. What they had said. What he had said. Silence would win him nothing and make him look guilty where he bore no guilt. Long ago he had forsworn violence, and he would keep his pledge. Those who lived by the sword died by the sword. The meek would inherit the earth.

But as he rode into his own lane and the small ranch house, where Gracie even now toiled ceaselessly, he worried that it wouldn't happen that way at all. Maybe Gracie had been right. For a moment he regretted ever saying a word about his past.

He watched the distant riders top a ridge and then descend out of sight, into the big valley where most of his cattle were grazing. It was their honor, not his, at stake.

Chapter 13

The branding season arrived, and that meant two weeks of brutal toil, dirt, discomfort, aching bones, and sleeplessness. Truman Jackson didn't mind. From the moment when his iron pressed his TJ brand into the left haunch of each of his calves, he was the undisputed owner of each calf.

The dozen ranches in the Cottonwood area shared the branding, moving from one ranch to the next until the whole spring calf crop in the district was branded, earmarked, and the bull calves castrated. All of this took a lot of labor, which was why the various ranches teamed up to get the job done.

At each place, the owner and his crew drove the mother-calf pairs into pens, and then the big crew set to work, some sorting out the calves from their bawling mothers, some keeping the irons hot, some wrestling the calves to the ground and pinning them while they were branded, and some of the boys gifted with a knife castrated the bull calves, turning them into steers. It was noisy, filthy work, in which everyone was covered with muck and manure. The only respite was a big noon dinner set out by the ranch wives, including Gracie.

The June days had slipped by quietly before branding, but Truman Jackson had not been fooled. Trouble would come. The family had no cash because the bank was exercising its thirty-day demand privilege, yet they made do. Stock salt was running low, and Heeber's feed store wouldn't advance them credit, but other than that the Jacksons had experienced no trouble. Truman had been able to borrow some salt from his other neighbors.

The work began, as always, with the Petersen and Marvine ranches, then moved to the Hines and Aller places, up to Heeber's and Jackson's outfits, and then over the rise into the next valley and Hobe Bandig's big place. Jackson had one of the smaller places, and had no employees other than himself and his sons, whom he brought. The boys were always handy around a ranch, and could rope a calf as well as men ten years older, but mostly they ran errands.

Jackson knew that these brandings would be a kind of test. His neighbors and their hands would accept him or not, be friendly or not. Within a few days he would know much more about his fate in Cottonwood. They all knew the whole story. They also knew he had been participating in these neighborly brandings for a dozen years. He had joked with them, sweated with them, shared meals with them, and made friends with all of them.

He showed up at the first place in a reserved mood, waiting for some sign that he would be accepted. But at least that first day, he hadn't any idea of what the men were thinking. It was all business. At the nooning he found himself isolated. But no one talked much anyway. Men were too tired, nursing aching muscles, too filthy, too eager to get the job done, to palaver much. So he downed beef and coffee and some of the women's fancy concoctions, and went back to work.

By the second day, over on the lush Marvine spread, things opened up a little. Glen Petersen joined Truman in separating heifers from bull calves and earmarking them for Del Marvine.

"Mighty fine thing you did," Petersen said quietly, out of the blue, when they had a moment's breather.

"Had to. That's just the start. I've sent letters out. From now on, some of my profit's going to pay people back."

"You were just a kid. A horse holder."

It's just something I have to do, Glen. Then I'll be a free man."

"You're a free man now, Truman. Some are worrying a little about you, but I've told 'em all that a man who talks about a past no one knew of, and puts it all on the table when there's not one charge against him, that's the most honest man in the neighborhood. Of course a few, they say once an outlaw, always an outlaw, as if a man can't change."

"Glen, you're a mighty fine neighbor," Truman said.

"They make trouble, Truman, you call on me. I'm plumb wildcat when I get mad."

"Thanks, Glen. I'll see if I can do it alone. I think it'll blow over soon. Quail's got letters and wires out, and the bank and some others . . . giving me some trouble. But I think this is a good place to be, and Cottonwood'll take care of me right. And I'm not planning to leave Cottonwood now or ever."

That was all that was said, but it was plenty. He had a friend.

By the time they had gathered and branded at the Hines ranch and Aller's Lazy-A outfit, the ice had melted. Most of the boys were just waiting to see if the man they had known so long was any different now than he was last time they saw him.

The dawns were the most social. By nightfall they were all so weary that they washed, ate, and fell into their bedrolls. Sometimes they just fell asleep without eating or washing at all. But in the mornings, when they were collecting the horses, saddling up, squatting around a camp kitchen sipping scalding coffee, the stockmen relaxed and enjoyed themselves.

More of them asked Jackson questions, and Jackson answered each as honestly as he knew how. Yes, he had grown up the son of a notorious outlaw, mostly hiding in a box canyon, learning to hate the world and rob it. Yes, he had been a youthful helper, unknown to the law right to the end of the gang. He described in detail his flight from Montana Territory, and his quest for a better life.

"You want us to call you Will?" asked Jake Hines.

"No, Jake, Will Dowd's buried, no longer a person, no longer a boy full of trouble. You've always known me as Truman Jackson. It's a pure invented name. I don't know why I chose it, except it sounded opposite of everything I'd known. I'd be pleased, if you still want me around here, to be called by the name you've always hung on me."

"Some of us don't quite get it, Truman. You had no one chasing you. You could just keep quiet the rest of your life, and no one would ever know. But now you got trouble. Old Quail, he's itching to pin something on you. You must have known that would happen. There's a bunch here that can't reckon why you come out of hiding like this."

"Jake, it's simple. I had to do what's right. I know pretty much everything about you people; you have a right to know everything about me. Now you do. Once I did that, and once I decided to try to pay back the people who got robbed, then I'll be done, and square. I'm not square with the world until I've done all I can."

"Well, there's some here that don't get it, but I do, and I plumb admire it."

Most of the men sipping bitter coffee that morning nodded. A few just stared. There would always be some who'd think an outlaw would never be anything else, and Cottonwood would be better off driving him away. Truman could now begin to sense who was with him, and who wasn't.

There were only half a dozen to worry about, Heeber chief among them. Arch Understreet, the association detective was another. That man was paid to uncover crime, unlike a lawman, who was paid to do justice. Understreet had been on hand the whole gathering, studying brands, looking like he ached to find criminal evidence to throw at Jackson. Then there was Welch, not a likable man in any case, furtive and silent and thinking loud thoughts; and Staples, the rancher farthest away, was a strange distant man who maybe mavericked a few himself, slaughtering neighbor beef for his own kitchen. He was glad now to have another suspect around Cottonwood to ward off attention to his own doings. Maybe one or two more. Jackson was gauging them all by their stares.

The weather held, and the branding operation moved to Weber Heeber's huge place, and they began work on his shorthorn herd. Heeber's outfit would take three days and three campsites before they had his mark on twenty-seven hundred calves.

They were all exhausted now, though less than halfway through the work. Heeber profited the most from the roundup, because he had the most calves to brand and castrate and earmark, and consumed the most of the free labor. But no one minded, and most of the ranchers figured it was best to stay on the good side of the owner of the bank, the board member of the Utah Stock Growers Association, and the owner of the feed store. So they pitched in, Jackson among them, cutting out red calves, dragging them to the branding fire, frying his Flying W into their tender flesh, cutting, earmarking, and then letting them scamper back to their bawling mothers.

They arrived at last at Jackson's modest spread, and set out at once to gather his herd from the four sections of the ranch. It was by far the most beautiful ranch in all of Cottonwood, but the cowboys scarcely noticed. The configuration of a good horse might catch their eye, but not the noble slopes of the Uintas.

The work went swiftly. These ranchers had long experience with each place on the circuit, and their men knew how to chouse cattle out of tough corners just as well as the Jacksons did. The bawling mass of cattle eventually reached a paddock near the log ranch house, and the boys got down to the branding, using Jackson's TJ iron.

Jackson was expecting to brand about a hundred calves, dogies of all shapes and descriptions. His was a ragtag herd, gathered every which way. The rest were cows, unbred yearling heifers, yearling steers, bulls, bull calves, and a few dozen lame or injured or sick-looking specimens destined to be culled from the herd and shipped.

When trouble came, it was so subtle that Jackson didn't recognize it at first. There in the herd was a Flying W shorthorn cow and calf. That was normal. The boys put Heeber's brand on the slick calf. Then another. And a third. More fence jumpers than usual from the big outfit next door.

That was odd. Jackson had ridden those two fences—the Heeber spread joined two sides of Jackson's ranch—and they had been sound just before the gathering. He would check again as soon as he could.

By the end of that day, eighteen Flying W pairs had been discovered amid the Jackson herd. Each calf was duly branded with Heeber's mark, and the eighteen strays were driven to their home range by a gaggle of young cowboys.

It wasn't an accident. Someone had driven them onto the Jackson land just before the gathering. There wasn't anything illegal in it. Just strays. Nothing like a blotched brand or a calf bearing a TJ sucking on a Heeber cow. But just irregular enough to sow the seeds of suspicion.

And Truman Jackson knew, suddenly, that the association's blacklist would soon include his name.

And who would remain a friend once that happened?

Chapter 14

The quiet days of summer slid by, and life seemed almost normal to Truman Jackson. But it was an illusion. He got around the bank easily enough by selling a calf to Jake Hines, who paid cash for it. Smith's Mercantile didn't turn down Gracie when she paid for goods. Not even the feed store objected when Truman laid out cash for stock salt.

But things weren't right. More and more people were shunning him, which was the opposite of what he expected. He had earnestly believed that once people thought about the man who had been their friend and neighbor for a dozen years, they would see the man, not the boy outlaw, and life would go on.

He could not walk into the post office without being hectored by Horatio Bates, who wanted to know every detail, every slight, every hopeful sign. At least Bates declared himself in Truman's corner, and professed to admire his courage. That was more than most people in Cottonwood had done.

One July morning, Bates flourished a letter.

"Here. First reply," he said omnisciently.

The postmaster sounded so positive that Jackson wondered whether the man had steamed the envelope open.

This one was from Helena, from someone Jackson had never heard of, a Mabel Guilder. Jackson slit open the envelope and read the note.

"Dear Mr. Jackson,

"Your letter certainly surprised me. I am the daughter of Eva Polarski, who was robbed in seventy-three by the Dillin-Dowd Gang. She never stopped talking about it. She died three years ago.

"From newspaper accounts and what she told me, I know that she lost $27 in cash, a gold wedding band, and a filigreed silver woman's watch pinned to her bosom. She always said she'd lost a hundred dollars, which was everything she and my father, a miner, had.

"If restitution could be made, that would be a most welcome and surprising event in my life.

"Mrs. Bosco C. Guilder."

Jackson handed the letter to the postmaster.

"That's a lot of money, Truman."

"Yes. In a good year we clear a thousand. In bad years we clear just enough to live on." He sighed. "We'll be spending a lot of time paying these back."

"Admirable, admirable, but you were exactly one-sixth of that gang, and a boy. Maybe you should pay one-sixth."

"Every last cent. Make things right. It's something I have to do."

Bates turned to help half a dozen others who had flooded in, and Jackson pierced into the dusty street and blinked his eyes in the glare. The State Bank of Cottonwood loomed on the corner, and he walked toward it, his boots raising whirls of dust in the sunbaked boulevard. He stepped into shade on the boardwalk, and entered. He hadn't been in the place since they had refused to let him cash a small draft.

He didn't bother with Bob Scott, but headed straight for Elton James's office.

The bank president, coatless in the heat, peered up, looking less than pleased.

"Please read this, Elton."

Jackson dropped the letter before the bank officer, who picked it up as if it were poisonous, and read through it.

"Well?"

"I want a draft drawn for a hundred dollars and sent to her."

"Well, ah, that's most admirable, Truman, this sudden change of heart, but we can't. You know, the sources of your funds are still under investigation and so we—"

"By who?"

"Why, we're awaiting word."

"Who is waiting word?"

"From Weber Heeber and the sheriff."

"About what?"

"Well, ah, whether—" James was sweating and chewing on his words as if they were wormy flour.

"Whether after twelve years here ranching as honestly as I know how, with everything backed by receipts and bills of sale, you can pin anything on a boy outlaw."

"You don't need to raise your voice with me."

Jackson leaned over the desk. "I want a draft for a hundred dollars now. Not thirty days from now. I want to right a very old wrong. Are you going to keep me from doing the right thing?"

" Well, I agree it's a nice gesture, and would sit well with people, which is what you want, I suppose, but I'm the instrument of the board of directors, and I can't just—"

Jackson wrestled down his rage. "All right. I'll write a draft right now, and in thirty days you'll honor it."

"Well, ah, you see, we may not be allowed . . ."

"Allowed by who?"

"The sheriff . . ."

Jackson held his peace. The more he argued with the bank president, the less likely he would be to release the funds. "Very well," he said. "This is something worth talking about."

"No, no, don't misunderstand, Jackson."

"I understand maybe better than you know, Mr. James."

"You'd be wise to keep this under your hat—for your own good, Truman."

Jackson smiled, nodded, and stepped outside. He peered up and down the deserted avenue. The heat had chased people indoors. He still loved this place, his only home, even if the town seemed unwilling to help him take the final step.

He strolled slowly up the boardwalk, paused at

the offices of the *Cottonwood Advertiser*, and stepped in. Harlan Wood, the editor, was bent over a composing table, alone, so Jackson let himself through a small gate and into the ink-stained printing area.

Wood looked up. "Jackson," he said uncertainly. "What can I do for you?"

"Oh, nothing much. You know this town better than anyone. What's the verdict?"

"Verdict?"

Jackson nodded. "About me," he added.

Wood ran a hand through his thinning gray hair. He looked as if he hadn't seen sunshine for twenty years. "I don't know much," he said.

Jackson thought that Wood knew a great deal more than he was letting on. "Well, if you don't want to talk, I will. I got a letter today."

He thrust it at Wood, who read it.

"What's that all about?" Wood asked.

"At the potluck I not only told people what I was as a boy, I told them I was going to make an effort to pay people back. This is the first letter I got back. I will pay this woman what her mother lost."

Wood nodded. "I guess I remember that part of it."

"Only thing that's stopping me is the bank. I've three hundred in my account, but they won't let me withdraw any. Thirty-day demand, they call it, but actually they're seeing whether it's all loot from robberies . . . after twelve years of ranching here. So, at this point, I'm trying to pay this woman, and I can't. Board of directors won't let me. How's a man supposed to remedy wrongs if he can't?"

Wood pursed and unpursed his lips. "I suppose the bank's just being careful," he said.

"Care to write about it?"

"No, I don't care to."

Jackson smiled. "Will you ever?"

"No, I'm not going to touch this story."

"Do you think this town's going to let me live here?"

"Don't come to me with your problems, Jackson."

"Would you like to see my ledgers, going back every year Gracie and I've been here? Want to talk to my neighbors? How about Eli Pickrell? He's a man who knows my soul about as good as anyone."

Wood frowned, puttering with his type stick.

"I'm making you uncomfortable, I guess. The paper depends on advertisers. Advertisers depend on the bank, and so do you. I don't suppose you're very interested in one man's voluntary confession and redemption."

"You've got it all wrong, Jackson. I care."

"Then, you have a story to write. Try talking to Elton James at the bank, and ask him why a man can't try to remedy an old wrong."

"I'm busy. Got to finish this story."

"What's that about?"

"Weber Heeber says Cottonwood needs more law enforcement, a couple more constables, and the county should hire two more deputies. He says it's time to keep an eye on undesirables because there's some mysterious losses around the area."

"You believe that?"

"No reason not to."

"Rather a coincidence, isn't it?"

"I'm for justice. If there's trouble, we need more law enforcement. Now, I've got to get to work."

Jackson nodded. "All right. Thanks for listening. It's your conscience you're dealing with."

Trouble. His heart sank. He wondered whether this righteous little city was going to drive the Jackson family right out of town.

He thought of a way to pay the woman off if Jake Hines would help out with some greenbacks. Four calves would raise around a hundred. Enough to buy a postal money order from old Bates, and send the woman her due. It didn't matter what Cottonwood thought: This transaction was really between a man named Jackson, and his God.

Chapter 15

Styles Quail picked up a dozen manila envelopes and a few letters from the post office and found the postmaster in a talkative mood.

"You've a heap of mail from Montana Territory and Wyoming," Horatio Bates said. "You dug up anything on Jackson yet?"

"I'm leaving no stone unturned," he said. "Trouble is, the gang was shot down or put away long ago. But if there's anything outstanding on Jackson, I'll nail him."

"Why would you want to do that? He's been a good man, far as I can tell."

"If a man's committed a crime and goes unpunished, then justice is not done."

"Seems to me a man can redeem himself with good living. He didn't have to reveal his past, you know."

"Criminals are dumb. You have to be stupid to get on the wrong side of the law."

"That's not my point. He's revealed his past as the way of finishing up a long spiritual journey."

Quail was getting annoyed with the nosy post-master. "That doesn't mean a thing."

He stepped into the sunlight, examining his mail. There were thick brown envelopes from several sheriffs and county attorneys, and maybe there would be something interesting.

After Jackson had made his amazing confession, Quail had sent out nineteen letters in all, each describing the self-confessed Will Dowd, gang member, and asking whether there were warrants outstanding.

So far, the result had been disappointing. No one had ever heard of the kid, and nothing was outstanding, and in any case, the statute of limitations had precluded doing anything about any robbery.

The sheriff hiked through a blistering day to his cool jailhouse, and began sorting out the envelopes that interested him, all of them with Wyoming or Montana returns. Then he settled his sweating body into his creaky swivel chair and began examining the latest crop.

Most of the lawmen, and in some cases county attorneys, expressed no interest. Some included a typed copy of the indictment against other gang members. A couple wanted more information on Jackson, especially whether he had engaged in crime in Utah. Dead-end stuff. Quail knew there was little chance that it would lead anywhere.

Names of dozens of victims popped out of the material, though, and Quail debated whether to turn these over to Jackson, as the man had requested. On reflection, Quail decided not to. Jackson's restitution game was just showmanship. Jackson had a show-off streak in him, a regular Buffalo Bill Cody streak, thumping his chest and telling the world what a fine gent he was. Nah, say nothing to that crook. All those efforts to pay off victims would get in the way of real, genuine, serious law enforcement, when it came right down to it. That sort of stuff played well to juries, which is why Jackson was doing it.

The next to the last letter in the heap was from someone in Green River, Wyoming, just on the other side of the Uintas. Quail ripped it open and read the note with increasing interest.

It was from Brand Neihardt, the Sweet Grass County, Wyoming attorney. In 1872 an express car had been robbed of the U.S. mails, money, and gold. The expressman had been shot and died two days later. The Dillin-Dowd gang had been implicated. If there was an unknown member of the gang now boasting about it, Neihardt wanted the name. He may have been an accomplice in a capital crime.

Oh, that tickled Quail. If you fish long enough, you usually catch something. He had been trolling from the morning after that potluck supper. Oh, this would be something, all right. Of course there were obstacles along the way, but they could be surmounted. Chief of these would be extradition. Wyoming would have to persuade Utah officials there was credible evidence to go ahead with it. Which there wasn't . . . but that wouldn't stop an experienced sheriff like himself.

Styles Quail thought he might just take the prisoner over there himself, with or without extradition papers. It wasn't but a hundred miles or so. He knew the sheriff over there, Wiley Slater, an old rival of his, and this would put him one up. He'd enjoy unloading a stagecoach bandit in Slater's lap.

He brewed a pot of tea, feeling mighty fine. Tea was his drink. He hated coffee, especially the vicious brew decocted by the deputies and left to eat through metal for days on end. But set some good Earl Grey before him and Quail was a happy man. Now, as the tea steeped, he pulled out his nib pen, uncorked his ink bottle, pulled out a sheet of county letterhead stationery, and set to work.

He was thus engaged when county supervisor Weber Heeber wandered in. The man had taken a sharp interest in the quest to bring Jackson to justice, and dropped by daily to see what Quail's inquiries were bringing in.

"Ah, Weber, we have him now. Look at this!"

Heeber took the letter thrust at him, carefully unfolded spectacles and propped them over his nose, and began to study Neihardt's inquiry. He set the letter down slowly, staring out the window.

"I don't know how you're going to get Jackson over there," he said. "There's only the man's testimony at a potluck dinner, and I don't suppose this attorney can make much of it, especially after about fifteen years."

"Just leave it to me," Quail said. "I just may deliver Jackson. It's not so far."

Heeber raised an eyebrow, but his smile betrayed other feelings. Quail was good at reading other men, and he read the county supervisor clearly.

"Don't do anything that stretches the law, Styles," Heeber said. "This is a delicate matter. Jackson's been here a long time. He has friends, and whatever he said, he said voluntarily at a time when no one suspected him of anything."

"Dumb cluck," Quail said.

"Maybe."

"He wants a list of the gang's victims so he can repay them, he says. Now that's theater."

"Maybe. Maybe he's trying to make amends."

"You believe that?"

Heeber smiled slowly. "Hard to say. I think he's playing both sides of the aisle. We had a good look at his stock during branding. Understreet did, at my request. Lot of red cows in there, shorthorn types. We couldn't prove anything, but we noted a lot of strays from my place on his range. I've decided that's enough. I'm on the stockmen's association quarantine committee, you know. We're acting."

"How does that work?"

"Five of us. We each can put names on the list. If there's no objection from the other four, the name goes on the list. Then we publish it. We don't accuse anyone of anything. Just request, politely, that members and associates don't do business with anyone on the list. Nothing's said that's overt, but everyone gets the idea. We're private, not public, and we're not bound by all the fancy rules of evidence you've got to satisfy.

"We put people on the list, and sometimes we take people off. Usually, anyone on the list folds up and heads for another state. They can't do business in Utah anymore. Can't sell cattle, can't buy cattle, can't get feed, can't get transportation to ship cattle to packinghouses. The railroads are the first to cooperate with us. They don't want to haul stolen beef."

"So when does all this happen?"

"Few days. I've wired the rest of the committee, putting Jackson on the list. Haven't heard back from two. But pretty soon I'll hear from them, and then we'll publish the revised list around Utah. That's it."

"What does Jackson do?"

"He's got no recourse. We starve him out."

"He could drive his herd out of the state, couldn't he?"

"Maybe, but he won't. That takes men, pasture, and a place to go."

"What's he likely to do?"

Heeber shrugged. "Nothing. Styles, you got any doubts about going after Jackson?"

"Maybe I should ask you the same question."

Heeber looked around the dark, stark office, with its gun racks, dented spittoons, battered desks, and barred door leading to the lockup. The jail stank.

"Sure I do. And you?"

"If I did, I wouldn't admit it to no one. Weber,

the man was part of a gang. Sure, he's got a nice wife and family and all that, but the law's the law, and it's got to be satisfied. I liked him until that potluck. I don't know what got into him. A man should keep his dirty linen to himself. We all got dirty linen, but you don't see real men hanging it out on the laundry line. They keep it inside. That's when I stopped liking him, when he didn't keep it inside.

"A man should never show his faults to the world. Not ever. It's a sign of weakness. Religion got into him and ruined him. We'd have never known about him. He has no record. But in one stupid moment he threw it away, and my respect went with it. So, to answer your question, I hardly got doubts anymore. He's weak, like all crooks." He smiled. "All right, now it's your turn."

Heeber didn't smile. "I just don't know. I got plenty of doubts. That Gracie, she's a sweetheart, and I hate to hurt her. Plenty nice family. The thing is, no one knows whether he's reformed or not. We can't read his mind. He talks a good story, paying everyone back, but who knows? I've spent a lot of time worrying about this, getting torn up by it.

"Sure, I've doubts. But I think there's no room for doubts in Cottonwood. We want people we have no doubts about, people we know, people whose parents and grandparents and brothers and sisters we know for three, four generations. Not people that come out of nowhere, with no relatives and no past. We don't want people like that around. We have to have trust. That good enough for you, Styles?"

"You're meaner than I am, Weber," he said. "All I care about's the law. It says a man's innocent until proven guilty. You've got him guilty until he proves himself innocent."

Chapter 16

Eli Pickrell knew what this was all about, and waited in the parlor of the white clapboard parsonage. The Community Church's governing committee was due at seven-thirty to discuss an important matter.

Pickrell, widowed and with adult children, lived alone, supplementing his small church salary with an insurance business. He liked to tell people he insured for every calamity in life, and in the afterlife.

He had a good idea what the church's governors would say, and he expected the division among them to run four to one, or maybe three to two, against Truman Jackson. This church was a democratic one. The issue would be taken to the general congregation, whose decision would be final.

They all filed in together only a few minutes late, as if they had gathered somewhere for a last-minute consultation before arriving at the doorstep of their minister. They exuded counterfeit good cheer and bland civility. Most laymen behaved peculiarly in the presence of their clergymen.

"Welcome, gentlemen," Pickrell said. "We can

meet right here. Chairs enough if two of you'll share the settee. I'll light another lamp."

They settled themselves into Monkey Ward mail-order furniture while Pickrell lifted the glass chimney, struck a match, touched the wick, turned it down until it gave a small clean flame, and replaced the glass chimney. The warm light struck the faces of five smiling, uncomfortable, middle-aged men, all of them prominent in Cottonwood, all merchants, ranchers, or professionals. None was an employed person.

"This is about Truman Jackson, I take it?" Pickrell asked. He didn't much care for hemming and hawing around.

"Yes," said Bob Sitgreaves, the church's moderator. "We consider this a grave matter."

"I consider it a joyous matter," Pickrell said. "There is rejoicing in heaven when just one soul is saved."

"Well, ah, that's the question," said Bertram Webb, who ran an undertaking parlor and furniture store. "The question is complex. You see, most of us aren't sure whether Jackson is sincere, or whether this is some sort of P. T. Barnum business."

Pickrell nodded. This, too, he had expected. It was not enough for a man with no charges against him for things done in his youth to come forth and reveal his past and try to make amends, and thus present himself to God and his neighbors as a transformed and penitent man. Not enough at all.

"We've broken it down into several items," said Carter Dawe, owner of Smith's Mercantile. "We all like Jackson. Everyone likes him, and Gracie, and the children. You'd get five votes here in favor of the proposition that Truman Jackson's quite a fellow. We're not hostile, or opposed or anything like that. We think the world of him. He'll probably have some exciting stories to tell his grandchildren someday.

"He's one of God's children, like the rest of us. But people are upset, you know. No one wants a stagecoach robber or worse sitting beside them. Our wives are quite alarmed, and looking to their possessions. Worse, the children think that bandits are exciting fellows, people to imitate. That's one trouble."

Pickrell smiled lazily.

"Another is respectability. Now, I know, this sounds a little like Pharisee talk, and position, and status, and all that, but it's not. It's about trust. You're a minister, and you'll understand all that. From the beginning, we've always been an honored part of this community. From our little church have sprung the leaders of Cottonwood. Many of the pioneers brought their parents with them, and the families of Cottonwood now extend through three generations. We trust each other. But suddenly there is distrust in our midst."

That sounded like Welsh, all right. Pickrell nodded, and then it was attorney Ebenezer Bunker's turn. "Now, Eli, we've looked into the theology of this. Not everyone's fit to be a member of the kingdom. Those who remain obdurate, unrepentant, aren't welcome. They're the lost. Every one of the branches of the faith, as far as we know, practices this. Excommunication, shunning, withdrawal of membership. This is done to protect the flock and preserve the doctrine."

"Well, yes. Mostly false doctrine, heresy. Sometimes an obdurate and unrepentant sinner. I can't think of any church who'd expel someone seeking to make things right with his neighbors and the Lord. He's begun the process of repaying the gang's victims. Are you going to expel him for that?"

"No," said Sitgreaves. "He's dodged the law for years, with a false identity. He's not Truman Jackson; he's Will Dowd, and that's ample reason. We invited Truman Jackson into the church, and now we find there's no one by that name, or by the name of Gracie Jackson. Let him serve time and satisfy justice. Let them both think about flying false colors. Then we'll see."

"I see. And is it necessary to protect the flock from Jackson? Is he the wolf in sheep's clothing? Has he invented heretical doctrine?"

"Well, ah, in fact, we think maybe the flock needs protecting. We're talking about a man who's lived a lie for twelve years. There is no Truman Jackson! You see, some of his neighbors, including Weber Heeber, a mighty fine Saint, think maybe he's not quite as reformed as he lets on. Now, nothing in our proposal to deny him membership keeps him from worshiping God in other venues or on his own. We aren't denying him anything."

"Except a couple of sacraments."

"Well, there's several churches and a few unorganized congregations in Cottonwood."

"I see. And what are the charges against Truman Jackson? Are they charges you feel are sufficient to keep him from our company?"

"Well, that he's a self-confessed criminal. That's ample in its own right. He came right out with it. And we've looked into Gracie, and she comes from a, well, boardinghouse."

"I see. He came here a dozen years ago. He and Gracie have belonged to this church for ten years. In all that time he's never been anything but an admired and exemplary member. Are you telling me a man never changes, never grows, never reaches out to God and his neighbors? Do any of you think what he did was admirable?"

Now they did look uncomfortable.

"We don't think he's ready. Maybe someday, but not now."

"Are you ready?"

"Me?"

"Yes, you. Let him who is without sin cast the first stone, eh?"

Bunker glared. "I have never strayed. I certainly admit to petty wrongs, God forgive me, but I have never robbed banks and trains and killed people."

"Well, maybe a boy horse-holder for a gang consisting of his elders didn't, either."

"That's for the law to decide, Eli."

"Ah, I see. You're in contact with Styles Quail. Suddenly it's not the church's beliefs that count here, but the law of the land."

"Well, yes, as a matter of fact. This man is probably wanted, or will be, which is a prime reason to expel him."

"A prime reason to admit him, I'd say. Here is where he finds help and succor in a time of trouble."

"Well, we appreciate your idealism, Eli. But we are practical men, and see things more realistically. If he had come to us ten years ago and said his name was Will Dowd, and he had a criminal past, and wanted to find the Lord and change his ways, who would have objected? No one. But he came to us as Truman Jackson, truly the wolf in sheep's clothing."

One of those pregnant pauses followed. The men were assessing him, and not kindly.

"Tell me," Pickrell said. "How did your vote go?"

"Four to one for removal," Sitgreaves said.

"And who resisted? Was it you, Mr. Wick?"

He nodded, looking uncomfortable. He was the youngest, the lowliest, a barber.

"Why?"

"There is nothing against him. And we should be more charitable. Truman's a fine man, and Gracie's a sweet lady, and we need people like that."

That took courage. Pickrell smiled, but didn't comment. That sort of assertion could mean that Wick would lose custom among the men in town. But it hadn't stopped him.

"Good. You've made your stand and so will I. Now, what do you have in mind, Bob?"

"A general meeting of the congregation, following Sunday services on August one. We'll put it to a vote. I'll announce it next Sunday."

Pickrell refrained from saying what passed through his mind; that if they expelled Truman Jackson, they would have to find themselves a new pastor. It occurred to him that he had failed, mightily. All his years in Cottonwood had been for naught. He could not conceal the bleakness of his own failure.

"One more question. Gracie and the children are members of this congregation. Are you going to propose to expel them, too?"

"We don't think we'll have to. If Truman is expelled, his family will follow."

That's how it went for a few more minutes, except for one more thing. Just the slimmest, vaguest hint, but there, nonetheless.

Carter Dawe hinted at it: if Eli Pickrell made an issue of it, perhaps the church would invite a new pastor to shepherd the Cottonwood flock.

The Reverend Mr. Pickrell didn't mind the threat so much as the sense of failure it engendered. Had he failed, over all these years, to touch the hearts of his people with the teachings of his Lord?

Chapter 17

It should have been the best time of day. The sun had slipped behind the Uintas, turning the heavens gold. The day's heat was bleeding away into the zephyrs. The mountains formed a dark rampart that promised cool. Gracie and Nell had finished their chores, and Gracie wanted nothing more than to sit on their veranda and find peace. The boys were down on the river, and Nell was in the barn playing with the cats.

But there was no peace. Truman had become moody and withdrawn, and now he sat in a home-made chair, staring into space. She knew his thoughts were bleak. She settled in the other chair beside him, but he didn't seem to notice. She wanted to talk with him, open up the subject that was wounding him, as one would lance a boil. But she couldn't think of a thing to say.

So they sat, their minds not on the idyllic panorama before them, but on the perversity of humankind. She had been the practical one who had said, Don't do it; don't tell. He had been the idealistic one who had argued, I need to take this final step to be in harmony with my neighbors and God. Now the roles had reversed. She was enormously proud of him, honoring his courage and trust to go forth with the transformation, now complete, that had made him a new man. She believed things would work out; people would not do him evil.

As she sat next to him, she thought that their relationship had changed. When they were young and desperate, it was "us against the world," and the dangers threw them together with such intensity that they became one. They had both mistaken it for love. She had been a she-cat protecting him, but in truth she barely knew him, barely understood the Will Dowd she was so ferociously protecting. And he didn't know her very well, either. They were too busy surviving.

They waded through what they utterly believed was a mean world, beset by people out to get him. Everyone was crooked, so why shouldn't they be? People just managed to hide their meanness behind a veneer of respectability. They had found no love, no kindness, no charity anywhere, and so they clung together, two allies in a vicious land, hiding Will's past, pretending to be just a couple of young people making their way along the frontier.

They didn't even think about love. They made jokes, and he liked her, and she liked him, and the whole world was against them. She couldn't date the beginning of the change, but it came.

Paradoxically, they had quarreled a lot and threatened to split up, but the instant danger emerged, they were thrown together again until the trouble passed. That's when she realized it wasn't love; they were just two strays fighting the world side by side.

Love came later, when they stopped hating the world. As soon as they trusted the world a little, they trusted each other. She could not place the moment when she knew that Will loved her and she loved him. But it was after they had arrived in Cottonwood, and found a home and a future in the sleepy Utah town. Maybe about the time she became pregnant.

Now she felt as though a whirlpool was sucking them under, drowning them, destroying everything they had reached for, and touched.

"Truman? Let's talk."

"I'm Will."

She steadied herself. Not that. Anything but that. Not Will, the outlaw, who thought the whole world was more vicious than he was.

"No, you're Truman, and I love you."

"Always Will. Why did I ever think I could escape? Why did I even want to?"

At least he was talking. That encouraged her. She stood, pushed her chair closer to his so she could capture his work-roughened hand. He didn't resist.

"We've come far. Let's not give up hope now."

"I've never given up hope. I just thought maybe the people in Cottonwood practiced what they preached, and believed what their ministers taught them. They're just as rotten as everyone else."

"That's what Will thought, but it's not true. Many people admire you and defend you."

"Who?"

"Most of them. I'd bet my last penny they do."

"But not the sheriff or the biggest rancher or the most important businessmen. Weber Heeber just wants this ranch. He doesn't care if we're hurt. He' s the most respectable man in Cottonwood, but that doesn't keep him from pushing his cattle into my fields at branding time to raise a few doubts."

She didn't have a reply to that.

"We robbed trains and stagecoaches; they just rob people other ways."

"Truman, you don't really believe that."

He sighed. "I don't know what to believe."

"Truman, you do know what you believe."

"They're going to whip us, Gracie." He squirmed restlessly. The light was fading. "I guess you'd better holler at the boys."

"They're all right. We're the ones who're fishing."

"They're going to take everything away from us and drive us out. Maybe put me away."

"I know," she said. "But not everything. You'll have me. Wherever you go, I'll go. You have our children. They'll come with us on this journey."

"If they send me away, you better forget me. Find someone to marry and raise the children."

"Truman! We shouldn't think like that. We've learned to have faith. We've learned that we're not alone on this earth. We've learned that most people are good, and help is always at hand if we ask for it."

"You have more faith than I do," he said. "I

thought that way until everything went bad. I thought people would welcome a man who was taking the final step and trying to pay for the things he did wrong. I thought most people would, anyway. But I was wrong. This is just another rotten little hole."

She thought he was going to rage at her. His face clouded darkly, but then he softened.

"You know, I can't be Will again after all," he said. "Not even if I tried. That kid didn't know much except how to be mad and afraid. Gracie . . . whatever happens, just know that I love you. If they put me in the pen, I'll love you. If they drive us from here, I'll love you. If we're separated, I'll love you. If I die somewhere, far from you, my last thoughts will be of you. You're the only reason I'm not Will Dowd. You're the only reason I keep on."

She touched his weathered cheek with her hand, and then ran it across his muscled shoulder and down his arm. It was answer enough.

He had swung back and forth this evening, sometimes thinking like the boy he had been, sometimes standing on the ground they had won together. She wondered if he could summon the strength and moral courage to just keep on going along the paths they had decided to follow.

As dusk settled, she saw the boys clamber up the path from the river. They had been shielded from the taunts of schoolchildren this summer, but when the next term started, they would suffer.

"There's the other reason I can't be Will," he said. "I don't want them being like that. I got it from my father and grandfather and mother and cousins. They all thought like outlaws, angry and scornful. We've got the boys going along our path. They'll never know how I grew up. When we heard someone riding up, it didn't mean good company; it meant we should close the shutters and pull out our guns."

The boys paused on the porch, and she surveyed them. Parker had torn his pants. She was about to scold, but the pressure of Truman's hand in hers stayed her.

"Stay here a minute, boys. Then you can wash up."

Jon and Parker settled on the stoop, looking restless.

Moments later Nell appeared, carrying a kitten. She, like the others, knew to return to the house when it grew dark.

"Well, now," Truman said. "I think we'll be going into Cottonwood on Sunday. We should go more often. But we'll go. Now, there's something you should know. Some people in the church don't much like our being there."

"Why's that?" Jon asked.

"That's a long story I'll tell you soon. It's my fault, not yours or your ma's. All my doing. And that's what I want to say. If people don't much care for me, don't you think something's wrong with you. It's not. We'll just go worship as we always do, and be thankful for all we have here—this place, the cattle, the sheep and dogs and cats, and most of all, each other. I think that this'll blow over pretty fast, and everything's going to be fine. And if anyone treats you bad, you just tell me quietly and we'll talk about it."

"What did you do, Pa?" asked Parker.

"It goes back to when I wasn't much older than you, and I was mixed up with some people that were doing things wrong. But that was long ago, and when I told people in the church, some didn't like it, but others did and said they were closer to us than ever. Well, that's all I've got to say tonight. Tomorrow we'll fix the fence, so get some sleep."

They drifted into the dark log house. They would light no lamps this midsummer's eve, and soon would be asleep.

"Nothing I can say's going to prepare them for this," he said.

He was right.

Chapter 18

Deputy Sheriff Hamlin Henshaw despised his boss, Styles Quail. Up until that famous potluck supper, which Henshaw had attended, he had no opinion at all about the sheriff. The man did his duty and did it well, and Cottonwood knew a sleepy peace, year in and year out.

But all that changed when Truman Jackson, at a church gathering, revealed his past—and his wish to take the final step into the community, and even repay those who had been hurt by the old gang, so long ago.

That brave revelation touched something deep in Henshaw's soul. Jackson had been an acquaintance and member of the congregation; now, suddenly, he was more. In Henshaw's eyes Truman Jackson was a genuine hero, a man who had pulled himself out of youthful trouble and into a good and honest life. And now he had taken the last step, at obvious risk to himself and his reputation. What more could man or God ask?

So it came as a nasty surprise that not everyone saw it that way, and an even darker surprise that

Sheriff Quail had concluded he had a criminal in his snares and was writing every lawman in two states about it. Quail was going to find some way to throw one of Cottonwood's finest citizens in jail, and that appalled Henshaw so much that he spent his nights worrying about it, seeking ways to stop this travesty of justice.

Quail had shown those letters to Henshaw, and in not one of them did the sheriff mention that Jackson was now a fine citizen, or that Jackson himself had revealed his past, as part of a long process of redemption. Neither did Quail mention in all that correspondence that the man wanted to repay the victims of his father's gang. No, that didn't count. At least not with the sheriff. But it counted with Henshaw, and other thoughtful citizens of Cottonwood.

Quail had an answer to that: "I don't care what he is now. The law has to be satisfied. He was an accomplice, and old enough to know better, and that's enough to put him away for years."

Henshaw had heard that a dozen times, mostly when Quail was responding to angry citizens, including the postmaster, Horatio Bates, and the Community Church's minister, Eli Pickrell. Both men had walked away disturbed and disappointed. Henshaw couldn't walk away; the sheriff's office was where he worked, and the way he supported his young wife and their first child, Billy.

Then, one by one, responses found their way back to Quail, as sheriffs and county attorneys in Montana and Wyoming let him know that they had nothing on Will Dowd, didn't know the boy had existed, and in any case the statute of limitations had run out. Henshaw began to have hope. No one cared.

Then the letter from the Green River County attorney Neihardt arrived, and everything changed. Quail thrust in front of every deputy on the force. "Now we've got the bastard. Make sure he doesn't pull out of here in the night. That time the gang murdered an expressman. No statute of limitations on that one. If Jackson was holding the horses for that one, we've got him."

Henshaw listened to that with a deepening gloom, but stayed quiet. He knew Quail would fire him in an instant if he opposed the sheriff in any significant way. Quail didn't like to be crossed. But the injustice of it haunted Henshaw, and led to sleepless nights wondering about the very nature of justice, and mercy, and forgiveness and redemption. For the first time in his young life, a chasm had opened between what he believed and what the sheriff and other lawmen believed about justice.

Quail wrote the Wyoming prosecutor at once, saying that Jackson was openly talking of his youthful crime spree as Will Dowd, and living on a ranch outside of town. If Wyoming wanted him, it would be easy enough to extradite him, and it was not a long trip to Green River, either.

It fell to Deputy Henshaw to take that letter, and other official mail, to the post office.

He handed the half dozen letters to Bates, and

waited for Bates to pluck up whatever was in the sheriff's pigeonhole.

"There it is, Hamlin. Few more replies from Montana. I guess old Quail's going to nail Jackson."

"Already has," Henshaw mumbled. "This here letter—the one to Brand Neihardt at Green River—that's going to do it."

Horatio Bates glanced at it. "Ah, county attorney up there."

"That was the next-to-last robbery by the gang," Henshaw said. "They killed an expressman. Right in the station, not twenty miles from anywhere. Bold as can be. That's a capital crime, Horatio. I'm afraid Quail's got him."

The postmaster sighed. "You like that?"

"No, I don't. I think a man that's been living right as long as Jackson ought to get a break. A man who wasn't even suspected of a thing."

"Wyoming's gonna extradite him? Papers from their governor to our governor to Quail, something like that?"

"I guess. That's what the sheriff says."

"But our governor doesn't have to go along with it, does he?"

"If there's good reason not to."

"Well, there's good reason."

"Quail doesn't care."

"Maybe he hasn't thought it through, Hamlin."

"When his mind's made up, it's made up."

"It's enough to make a man write our governor. I guess I'll just do that, soon as I hear that Jackson's being extradited. A postmaster carries a little weight, sometimes. Not much. But my letter's going to get read in the governor's office, and I'm going to tell the whole story so well that they'll think twice, there in Salt Lake. Maybe if we all do something . . ."

The postmaster said no more, but Henshaw knew he meant every word he said. Bates wanted Henshaw to help Jackson.

Filled with melancholia, Deputy Henshaw toiled back to the courthouse laden with mail and guilt. If he did nothing, he would help destroy a good man who deserved not prison, but the lauds and esteem of every person in Cottonwood.

Deputy Henshaw knew himself to be an ordinary man, not fluent of tongue, not gifted with arguments, not a man of weight in Cottonwood. But as he walked up the avenue toward the courthouse square, he took heart. It was not so much whether he succeeded, but whether he tried, that would count in the Book of Life. And who knew? A man of strong conviction sometimes could bend even the intractable.

He spent the day rehearsing his arguments, and didn't approach the sheriff until the end of his duty, and then waited a while more until he could catch Styles Quail alone.

The sheriff had no private office, just a desk in a corner of a big bullpen where everything associated with law enforcement in Cottonwood County transpired.

"What do you want, Henshaw? I'm not giving raises today." Quail laughed at his own joke.

"I want to talk about Jackson."

"Dowd, boy, Dowd."

"I'm asking you to reconsider. He's been a fine citizen for as long as he's been here. Has a fine family. It doesn't seem just—"

"Just? Are we going to talk about justice?"

"Yes, sir. A man who's so transformed that he could bring up his past himself, well, sir, I think he deserves our applause."

"Justice? You have odd notions, Henshaw." The sheriff shoved back from his desk, until the deputy could see the man's thick belt, sagging under the weight of a six-gun.

"Here's justice: it falls on everyone equally without fear or favor. And that includes our pigeon out there on the South Fork."

"There's a greater justice, sir—"

"Oh, there is? Now, show me the statute, and you'll make a believer of me."

"You'll find it in the Bible, sir. There's rejoicing in heaven whenever—"

"This is Cottonwood, not heaven, and it is governed by the laws of the state of Utah. And Wyoming, where Dowd's little crime occurred, is governed by the laws of that state. Are you telling me to ignore the law, Henshaw?"

"A word from you to the Green River authorities, I mean about Jackson's conduct here—"

"Let me get this straight, Deputy. You're telling me to ignore the laws of two states so that an admitted criminal can escape prosecution. What sort of deputy are you? Didn't you swear an oath when I took you on? Are you going to go back on your word to execute the laws faithfully?"

Henshaw felt the withering blast of Quail's scorn, but stood his ground. "There are times to let matters stand. Jackson is not only a good man, but he's trying to repay everything the entire gang stole. He could just as well have offered to repay one-sixth of it, his share."

"So?"

"Doesn't that count for anything with you?"

Quail laughed, unexpectedly. "Guilty conscience at work, Henshaw. Most criminals, unless they're simple animals, have one. We use that to good advantage."

"No, sir, this man wasn't even suspected. He was a kid the gang didn't talk about. No one wanted him. Not one man in a million would step forth the way he did."

"Just shows how dumb he was, Henshaw."

"I believe this deserves public airing, sir. I think all of Cottonwood, city and county, should consider this. I think you should hear from people. Poor people, ordinary people like me. They all like Truman Jackson, or anyway most of them—"

"Dowd, Henshaw, Dowd. And no, the law is the law, and I'd be unfaithful to my badge if I let public opinion interfere with it or weaken it."

"Well, I'm going to take this to the public, sir. I don't think extradition on some old charge would sit well."

"You'll not say a word to anyone."

"What I do on my own time, sir, is my business."

The sheriff stared, and then smiled, catlike, slowly.

"You may think so," he said. "Go ahead and think so. In fact, I urge you to think so."

Chapter 19

Weber Heeber timed his trip to Cottonwood to co-
incide with the posting of the mail. Bates usually
had it in the pigeonholes around two-thirty if the
coach from Vernal was on time. Heeber was waiting for one last letter. Even if the letter didn't arrive, he thought he would go ahead.

He drove the buggy to town this summer's day
because it provided a hood against the wicked sun,
and because he could pick up a few items. From long
practice, he knew the length of the trip to town. What
varied were the dray horses. A slow nag could double the time it took to reach Cottonwood.

But today he harnessed his fleetest horse and
took off at a rip, intending to get on with it. Some
things just had to be done, and he was man enough
to do them. Pauline was brimming with dark disapproval, but her esteem was not something he
craved, so he ignored her.

He found Cottonwood half asleep in the midday
July heat, and pulled his buggy up at the post office. The horse, Old Sue, had a fine sheen of sweat
over her withers and stifles.

Pudgy old Bates, looking more disreputable each day, along with his official dominions, was just poking the last letters into their cubbyholes. He glanced at Heeber and withdrew three letters.

"I guess you got what you wanted," he said.

Heeber noted the envelope he was waiting for, from a director of the Utah Stock Growers Association, and squinted. "And what am I wanting, Bates?"

"Oh, I wouldn't know."

"I swear, if you don't quit reading the mail, I'll complain to Washington City."

"Only postcards, Weber. They're fair game."

"Well, I'd wager you steam open envelopes, too."

"No. But I see what comes into the mails, and what I deliver, and unless I'm dumb as a stump I draw some conclusions. A few weeks ago, you wrote most of the officers of your stockmen's association, and now you've got your answers back. You're going to blacklist Truman Jackson, or I'm not an observant man."

Heeber smiled suddenly. There was no sense riling up Bates. He knew everything about everyone in Cottonwood, and more than once Heeber had gotten some answers from Bates that he couldn't get anywhere else—especially how people felt about one thing or another the county supervisors were doing.

"Well, as long as you've got that figured out, I may as well tell you the verdict," he said, sliding a fingernail under the seal of the letter.

A moment later he had his answer. "Jackson's on

the list, Bates. I'll be posting a notice here right quick."

Bates paused in his sorting. "Are you sure you're doing the right thing?"

"That herd of his—it's got a lot of red cows in it, like my shorthorns."

Bates paused. "You know, over the last several years, Jackson has come in here, and every spring he's said a kind word about you because you've given him lame calves, or let him buy some bummed calves for a dollar. He said you're just about the kindest neighbor a man could have. I guess now some of those bum cows would have produced two, three generations more. Jackson told me if it wasn't for you, he didn't think he and Gracie could have made it."

The postmaster spoke so gravely and earnestly that Heeber couldn't meet his gaze. If God himself had hurled a javelin into Heeber's soul, he couldn't have done better than old Bates.

"Well, it's out of my hands," Heeber said, shortly, knowing it wasn't true.

"I think it's in your hands, Weber. All it takes is a quick rinsing."

"Damn you, Bates," Heeber said, and retreated into the withering sun.

Leave it to Bates to remind him of the ways he helped his neighbor get going. Well, it was too late for that. If Jackson had just kept his mouth shut, it would still be like that. Jackson did it to himself. Stockmen couldn't have a stagecoach and railroad bandit in their midst, and that was that.

But his conscience wouldn't play dead.

He stopped at the *Advertiser* next door and arranged for the advertisement, already set in type, to run, and also to have five hundred flyers printed. The ad and flyers all said the same thing: "The Utah Stock Growers Association herewith denies membership to the following persons:" Jackson's name was added to a list of about forty. It was both subtle and unsubtle. The ads and flyer made no overt accusation, but not a soul in Utah failed to grasp the meaning of the blacklist. From the moment of publication, Jackson could not openly sell so much as a calf, or buy stock salt or hay or feed grain. It was an economic noose intended to strangle suspected crooks and rustlers. It was a swift, silent way to drive them out of Utah.

He talked to Willie Studemeier, an apprentice at the paper, arranged for the ad to run in the next two issues, and okayed the printing.

"You got him this time, eh?" Willie asked.

Heeber sighed. "He did it to himself. No one got him. We just can't let someone like that live here."

That sounded pretty good, but somehow Heeber knew it was pretty shabby. He couldn't explain to himself why he was acting the way he was.

He hiked across Utah Avenue to the bank, and found it cooler within. The massive stone-and-brick edifice tamed the sun. He headed for the rear, where Elton James would be sweating over the ledgers. James had made a good president. Heeber, chairman of the board, had selected him, and was not disappointed. The bank was solid and paying its stockholders, primarily Heeber, a tidy sum each year.

James looked up. "I got some ice in the box. Go chip some and get a glass of lemonade and cool yourself down. What brings you in on a day invented in Hades?"

"I got the letter. I figured it'd come sometime soon. That's it, Elton. Now I've got him."

Elton James didn't look pleased. "You sure you're doing the right thing?"

"That's the second time I've been asked that. Bates asked it, but he's just the town busybody. I suppose I am. Sometimes I'm not happy about it, but I think Jackson did it to himself."

"How?"

"He should have just kept his mouth shut. Now there's hardly a man of property in the county who thinks his property's safe."

James frowned. "I don't like this," he said. "I don't like the bank's policy on this, either. Tomorrow the thirty days are up. That's as long as we can keep his funds. He'll be in for them. When he came in a month ago and wanted twenty dollars out of his account, I told him we were exercising our right to thirty days on demand. Then he switched and said he wanted to withdraw everything, over three hundred I guess. That's tomorrow."

"Well, find some excuse."

"There's no legal one."

"Well, find something. Or just say no and don't give a reason."

Elton James stared at Heeber. "Look, Weber, if

you want the bank to do something unethical or illegal, you had better hide it from the board. And if you or the board tells me to do something that is plainly wrong, I'll say no, and you can decide what to do about that."

Heeber secretly admired the bank president, who was showing exactly the integrity that commended him to that high position.

"Have the sheriff slap something on the account," Heeber said. "A replevin, anything."

"No, you do that. I won't. Weber, this is going to be a mess. If we mess with state banking law, we'll lose our charter. If word leaks out that we're keeping Jackson's own money from him, we're going to see a lot of folks close their accounts."

"We're the only bank in Cottonwood," Heeber replied.

"Western people have gotten along without banks for years. Any merchant with a safe can bank. Saloon keepers have been bankers. If people need a mortgage, they drive to the nearest banking town to get it."

Heeber sipped the delightfully chill lemonade, pleased to have such a rare treat on a fiery day, and contemplated that.

"I'll go talk to Quail. He can get some kind of court order. The man's a bank robber, so it shouldn't be hard to keep his mitts off the cash. And then we'll have him."

"Not we, but you. You'll have him."

"You on his side?"

"My mind's not made up. But it's a rare man that

tells about his past like that, when he isn't wanted by anyone, and offers to pay up the entire losses the gang inflicted on hundreds of folks for many years. A rare man. And he's been solid here, just as solid as they come. No, Weber. If you're going to play with the devil, you do it alone. I'll tell you one thing that's a caution. The board's restless. They're not happy."

Heeber knew that. He sighed.

"I'll go talk to Quail. He listens to county supervisors like me. I'll bring some legal talent, too. I don't know much about the law, but it shouldn't be hard to tie up Jackson's money with some kind of action. We'll talk it over, and it'll be the county's action, not the bank. Don't worry, the State Bank of Cottonwood's going to do nothing more than obey a judicial order."

James stood. "That's not right, Weber. It's just plain not right. Give the man his money."

"Maybe you're right, but it's gone too far. He should've kept his trap shut."

Heeber sucked the last of the lemonade and then rolled some ambrosial ice around his mouth, and headed into the heat.

Chapter 20

Truman and Gracie Jackson arrived in Cottonwood just about the hour the State Bank of Cottonwood swung open its double doors. He parked the buggy on Utah Avenue and helped Gracie down. Together they entered the bank, and steered directly toward Elton James's office.

James stood, greeted them, and got right to the reason for this visit.

"I've been expecting you. The thirty-day demand deadline has passed, and you'll be wanting your money. I'm hoping you'll change your mind . . ." He smiled amiably at them. "We hate to lose a good customer."

"We'd like our money, Elton," Jackson said.

James sighed. "All right, then. I'm hoping that when these difficulties pass, you'll reopen your account."

"I'm afraid we can't. Not with the current board."

James nodded. "Just a minute," he said, and left the office. He returned awhile later with some greenbacks and change in hand, and a ledger sheet and a form for Truman to sign. Then it was over. Jackson had over three hundred dollars in hand, that no banker could sit on for more than a month or decline to give back to him.

Jackson stuffed the cash into a small billfold and led Gracie into the shade-dappled street.

"That went better than I thought," he said.

He handed Gracie sixty dollars to pay off their account at Smith's Mercantile and pick up some groceries, while he walked over to the feed store for some stock salt. He hoped to get out of town and back to the ranch before the heat built up.

He stepped into the cool, pungent confines of the feed store and approached the counter. Andy Blitz, the cadaverous clerk, was acting twitchy.

"Hey, Andy, what's new?"

"Nothing."

"Another hot one, eh?"

Blitz nodded.

"I need some stock salt. A hundred pounds."

Blitz shook his head.

"What's the problem? Am I in arrears? I thought we paid this account a few weeks ago."

"You'd better go," Blitz said, his Adam's apple bobbing up and down.

"You ought to answer your customers' questions, Andy."

The young man seemed almost spastic. "Mr. Heeber, he said I can't sell nothing to you."

"Why?"

Blitz nodded toward a pillar. Posted on it was a fresh notice bearing the heavy legend across its top,

UTAH STOCK GROWERS ASSOCIATION. Truman had read dozens of them in his life as a rancher, and knew instantly, without reading the text, that the name of Truman Jackson had been added to the blacklist, and that it was Heeber's doing. He was on the committee that made such portentous decisions, often without a publicly acknowledged reason.

Jackson had been expecting it, but the actuality hit him hard. The stockmen's association hadn't the slightest coloration of public law, and yet laid down a law of its own, and without the solid evidence that any court or other governmental agency would require.

Jackson would soon be out of business. That is what struck him forcefully as he stared at the broadsheet. He knew that even now, copies of that sheet would be en route to every town and courthouse in Utah.

An odd thought filtered through his mind. "All right, Andy, do I have any unpaid bills here? I'll square things up."

"I never heard of that. I'm not supposed to do business with you, that's what Weber said."

"Pull my account, Andy. What do I owe?"

Blitz nervously fingered through a card file, pulled the Jackson account, and studied it. "'Bout eleven dollars and twelve cents," he said.

"Imagine Heeber won't mind if I paid it," he said.

"I guess not."

Jackson peeled off some greenbacks, Blitz made some change and gave him a receipt.

Jackson stepped into the blazing day, and blinked. He felt trapped. He could no longer sell a cow in Utah, ship his stock elsewhere by rail, or buy ranch supplies. A neighbor who bought any of Jackson's stock would be subject to the blacklist as well. A butcher or packer who bought any of Jackson's cattle for slaughter would find himself boycotted. Some did, paying the desperate cattleman a half or a third of the value of an animal, and defied the boycott. The organization had no legal status as an enforcement agency, but its range detectives enforced its laws, working closely with sheriffs and county attorneys. The range detectives had plenary power to capture suspect cattle and turn them over to the association as allegedly rustled or mavericked beef. Which was about to happen to every animal Truman and Gracie possessed.

It wouldn't take long for the noose to tighten. The Jacksons probably would miss their annual mortgage payment, due October first of each year. Within a few months, the Jacksons would be penniless.

He stood in the street, feeling the blast of the sun, feeling numb and empty. This was his town, the place where he and Gracie had come to try to find a way out of darkness. This was where he had spent a dozen years, learning how to be a neighbor. This was where he had made friends, learned to love, and learned to set aside hatred and fear and excuses, and take responsibility for himself and his loved ones. But now the town glowered at him in the fierce heat, a sullen city waiting to vomit him into the wilderness. He felt the crush of aloneness steal back into him, the same friendlessness he knew as a boy when all the world was his enemy.

He walked heavily up the boulevard, unaware of passersby, thinking only of the disaster Weber Heeber had visited on him. Almost without realizing where he was going, he drifted to the courthouse, and then to the sheriff's bailiwick.

Quail watched silently as Jackson pulled off his broad-brimmed hat and sank into a chair.

"I guess you win, Styles," he said. "They've blacklisted me."

"That's not my victory, Jackson. My sole interest is to see that the law is enforced and justice is done. In fact, I don't relish what they did to you. I've known it was coming."

"I thought you'd be delighted."

"You don't understand me, Dowd. I'm not out to get you; never have been. But I sure as hell wish you'd kept your trap shut. That was the dumbest thing you've ever done. Made a lot of work for me. There I was, with a confessed train robber and gang member in my county, and I had to make sure you weren't wanted anywhere.

"Maybe you thought you'd gotten away with it. Old crimes, old times. But not for murder. I'm not accusing you of that; but you yourself said you were holding horses for men that killed. I wish to hell you'd just kept quiet and lived your double life, and then we could still be shaking hands at potluck suppers."

"I did what I had to. Nothing less would work."

Quail laughed. "You're about to be extradited to Wyoming, and stand trial for that gang killing in Green River. Brand Neihardt, the prosecutor there's been up to Deer Lodge, Montana, to depose your cousins. He said he didn't have enough evidence on your say-so. After that, assuming your cousins don't shut up or lie, which would add a few years to their time, you'll be sent up there. I don't like it. Why the hell did you do it?"

Jackson didn't reply. Between the extradition to Green River, and the stockmen's blacklist, he was in a tightening vise and soon Gracie and his children would be starved and miserable, and he'd not be seeing much sunshine for many years. He felt bone tired, defeated, and stupid.

"Let me tell you something," the sheriff continued. "Just so you know there's nothing personal. Heeber came in here and wanted me to phony up some reason to keep you from getting your money out of his bank. I don't care if he's a county supervisor. I told him there was nothing on you here, you're clean, and I'd be damned if I'd do something illegal or wrong just to put the squeeze on you.

"In fact, I told Heeber he was on the wrong side of the tracks and by God, he'd better quit because I enforce the law without fear or favor. And I meant it. I heard later from them courthouse lawyers that Heeber had tried to jigger up something against you so he could keep you from your funds. We don't like that around here. And I'm going to vote against Heeber next time around."

Jackson stared wearily at the sheriff. "You're a good man, Quail. I got you wrong."

Quail smiled slowly. "Don't be dumb, Jackson. You trust too much."

"Maybe I do. Well, I'm not going anywhere. What I started, I'll finish. You keep me posted. I need to do something for Gracie and the children, find them some way to live. They have no place to go. We have no relatives. I don't know what to do. I can't even sell a steer."

"You shoulda thought of that, Dowd."

"I did. I thought maybe Cottonwood would welcome a man trying to become a good citizen and friend. I guess you have to be born respectable around here."

Jackson closed his eyes a moment against the headache that was beginning to swell from the base of his skull, and sighed. "Just let me know," he muttered, and walked through the coolness of the building and into the blast of July heat.

It would be hell to tell Gracie.

Chapter 21

When the Reverend Eli Pickrell opened the door of the parsonage upon Truman and Gracie Jackson, his heart sank. He knew he would be utterly inadequate for the task awaiting him. What mortal could stop the whirlwind?

He ushered them into his threadbare parlor, which was no cooler than the furnace outdoors, and they sank into his horsehair settee.

"We'd like to talk with you. We're at our wits' end," Truman said. "Gracie and me, we're being hounded back to where we started from."

"I'm glad you came. Perhaps we can explore the Lord's will for you."

Jackson sighed, and Pickrell had a sense that the man's faith was running thin.

It took Jackson a long moment to compose himself. Then he described, in measured words, the morning's travails. The stock growers had blacklisted him. The prosecutor in Green River was preparing to extradite him. The feed store would no longer sell him stock salt or ranch supplies. He could not buy or sell livestock and thus had lost the means to support his family. The only bright spot was that, finally, Elton James had let him withdraw the balance of his account. That would let him weather another month.

But the deepest hurt of all was the rejection. People who had been good friends suddenly cold-shouldered Gracie and Truman Jackson.

"Shouldn't they trust us all the more now? Wasn't my potluck talk the very thing that the good Lord requires of us? We've tried so hard. Gracie's been by my side every minute. We're not the people we once were. We stopped being tempted long ago. Nothing would drive us back to the life I'd followed as a boy. Nothing. But now . . ." Jackson's thoughts seemed to fade into a cloud of melancholia.

"You've a right to be angry."

"We're not. We're just so disappointed. And we don't know what to do. All alone. I thought I'd never be alone again. I was always alone when the whole world seemed like the enemy. Now I'm alone again."

"We're all of us alone," Gracie said. "I can't put the children back in school. I'm not much of a reader, but I can do my sums, and I'll teach them at home as long as I can."

That was her way of saying they expected their ranch would be taken from them when the mortgage was overdue. Pickrell knew that this couple, who had struggled so hard, learned to live in new ways, learned not to hate and distrust the world, was on the brink of despair.

"You're the best thing that ever came to Cottonwood," Pickrell said. "You're the flaming sword of God, come to cleave this town in two. Mark my words. This town will come to honor you. You're transforming it, even though the people of Cottonwood are unaware of that. You'll shame weak people into behaving better, show the world that faith really counts, and galvanize the best people in town to defend and help and honor you."

"All we wanted was to be accepted by our neighbors as ourselves, and not someone else," Truman said.

"Yes, and you've achieved it, though you don't see it yet. You've more friends than you ever knew, and your friends are the kind of people I admire."

Pickrell gauged the impact of that on these two discouraged wayfarers along the path of life. He wanted to hearten them first.

"Let me tell you something," Pickrell continued. "You've passed 'em all by. You made yourself finer and better than most everyone who never faced what you faced, or started life the way you started it. When I first met you, I wondered about you. Chip on the shoulder sometimes. Not much trust of others. But as the years went by, that slipped away and the Gracie and Truman I admire so much right now emerged. Little did I know—no one knew—what you had overcome to arrive at the grace and graciousness within you."

"Well, it's all over," Truman said. "I thought maybe we might be accepted here. I guess I was just another fool."

"No, you two are the shining lights of Cottonwood. You may not believe it, or may not care, but you'll see. When this is over, Cottonwood is going to remember you as the cleansing force that turned this tranquil little place upside down and showed us all how far we have to go."

"And we won' t be here."

"Yes, you will. If there is good cause, our governor doesn't need to respond to Wyoming's extradition papers. We're going to give him the truth. Already people in this congregation are preparing to head for Salt Lake to lay the case before him."

"How many?"

"A half a dozen, and one of them is our deputy sheriff, Hemlin Henshaw."

Jackson pondered that. "What about the rest?"

"The rest are a sign of my failure as a pastor."

"Your failure?"

"There are things afoot that I cannot prevent. Bob Sitgreaves and the selectmen are going to call a meeting of the congregation following Sunday services August one, and the issue will be whether to expel you from the congregation."

"What have we done to be expelled?"

Pickrell sighed. "Exactly. What they don't know is that if they expel the most profoundly Christian man and woman in my flock, they expel me as well."

"You've said so?"

"No, I don't threaten. But they'll find out about it within a moment of the time that they ask you to depart from their midst."

"What is their argument?" Truman asked.

"Trust. They said that everyone in the church has always trusted others until now. Family, and all that. They said that they know the parents and relatives of other members, but yours are in prison or dead. Unity. They say as long as you're in the congregation, they can't worship with one heart and one mind and one purpose. They've even argued that people don't change, and you'll just go back to the old ways when things get tough, or when it suits you. A lot more like that, and not a thing about forgiveness, or repentance, or rejoicing that two people have found God. It was as if all my sermons landed on deaf ears."

That was hard news to visit upon crushed people, and Pickrell wished he could have softened the blow.

Truman Jackson stood tall and thunderous and grim.

"We can spare the church that by resigning," he said.

"No, don' t do that."

"We'll spare ourselves, then. I'll write it and send it to you. That'll be my resignation. It's up to Gracie to decide what she does. She can do whatever's best for the children."

"Wherever thou goest . . ." said Gracie.

"All right, then, Eli. Tell them they can abandon the meeting. As of now, we're out."

There was something in Jackson's voice that rang with iron and cold.

"Truman! Wait a minute. Are you doubting God?"

Jackson didn't reply.

"Are you doubting his goodness? His purpose? That he might be using you in a blessed way?"

Jackson stared at the reverend with such bleak and bitter silence that Pickrell cringed. Then Jackson drew Gracie toward the door. Pickrell thought he saw a man and a woman slipping away not just from the Community Church, but the Lord.

"Truman. Pray!"

But Truman Jackson had already slipped into some other world, and Pickrell knew that this last bit of news had crushed them both.

Jackson looked terrible. Great shadows circled his eyes. Fever seemed to beset him. A flinty hardness had settled into his face. This man, who had taken the bravest step toward grace Pickrell had ever seen in his years of ministry, was visibly falling away.

"Pray, pray!" Pickrell cried.

Jackson led Gracie to the door and opened it, his silence like a steel wall.

But then he paused. "We won't cause you any more trouble," he said sternly, and led Gracie into the blistering heat.

Pickrell stood on the stoop, reproaching himself, filled with a sadness that ran deeper and darker than anything he had known as a pastor of souls. He closed the door slowly, wanting to run out into the dusty street and plead with the Jacksons. But it would not do.

He retreated from the heat and slumped into the settee, feeling abject failure. It had been the news of the church meeting that had been the last blow, the last nail through the hands and feet of Truman and Gracie Jackson. And yet he had no choice but to mention it. It would have been utterly wrong to keep those terrible things from the Jacksons.

He covered his face, facing his own crisis of the soul. Had he done all he could? Had he gone out into his congregation, like a pillar of fire, to defend the Jacksons?

The heat oppressed him, and sucked energy from his body, and strength from his soul.

Truman and Gracie had made an incredible spiritual journey only to find the last hurdle too high for them. Cottonwood had turned an outstanding man and his beloved wife into pariahs. And maybe outlaws once again.

Chapter 22

Gracie waited for Truman to run some errands. He had parked the rig in the shade of a majestic cottonwood tree, where the eddying breezes could draw the heat away from her and the dray horse. She didn't mind. Eli Pickrell's news, that the Community Church would probably expel Truman, was sobering and she wanted to think about it.

The town she had come to love and trust was betraying them. And for what? For Truman's honesty. The minister was right—what Truman's announcement had done was shame the self-righteous and shake the comfortable old alliances, connections, and webs of respectability in Cottonwood. There were those in this little town who suddenly despised Truman, not for doing something wrong in the distant past, but for doing something so noble and right that they could no longer bear to look within themselves and see their own barrenness.

She could not fathom the future, so she didn't try. All that mattered was that they had done their best. Truman had taken the last step. Now it was up to God. They would not turn back. Neither she nor Truman had the slightest wish to live on the margins of society, suspicious, friendless, resorting to desperate measures to survive. They had come this far, and they would not retreat. She saw the gracious shaded streets of Cottonwood with a new vision. This little place only pretended to be Eden. But Cottonwood was hell.

She saw Truman return, bearing two bundles, and she wondered what he had purchased. She had already purchased everything they needed, using cash because Smith's Mercantile would no longer run a monthly account.

He settled the packages beside her, clambered into the buggy, and grinned. She hadn't seen him grin in weeks. When they left Mr. Pickrell's parsonage, his face looked like a hailstorm.

He lifted the reins and slapped them over the croup of the horse, which startled the animal out if its nap. The buggy lurched forward into the burning sun, and Gracie knew it would be a mean, parched ride home.

"Here," he said, handing her a soft and bulky package. She opened it and beheld an entire bolt of navy blue polka-dot gingham. "Make yourself a dress. Make something for Nell. Maybe some shirts for the boys."

"Truman!"

She treasured the gift. He was trying to lift her spirits. The fabric was so unexpected. She fingered the gingham, smelled its starchy freshness, and smiled at him.

"What's in the other?" she asked.

"Secret. Don't open."

"I can't stand secrets."

He grinned, and settled the sullen horse into a trot and turned the rig up the South Fork Road, passing through parched pastures that rose gently toward foothills. Beyond them rose the green, cool ramparts of the Uintas, towering thirteen thousand feet into the cobalt sky. She wished she could be up there in the sweet, fresh, pine-laden air beside a crystal stream.

The other package was solid, heavy, cylindrical, and mysterious.

"I'm going to take a peek," she said.

"Wait."

"You know that marriage vow, to love and obey?"

"Yup."

"Well, I'm going to break it."

She began laughing, and then he laughed, too, and when she had sufficiently melted his resolve, she plucked up the other package, unwrapped the butcher paper, and beheld a quart bottle of Old Crow.

"What is this?"

He smiled puckishly. "When there's nothing else to do, try a celebration."

"Truman . . ."

"Am I quitting? No. Am I going to have a drink tonight? Yes."

"But, Truman . . . we'll throw everything away."

"Why do you say that?"

"You're caving in. The pressure's too much. Just throw it out and we'll forget this."

He simply smiled. Reluctantly she set the bottle on the floorboards. It was a thing that had come between them, an unexpected enemy. The bottle rolled slightly whenever the buggy creaked over a pothole or rut.

"You've been through too much," she said. "The church business was the last straw."

He smiled. "I'm not going to have a drink because we're desperate. We'll have a drink because we've won. Eli Pickrell was right. We've shamed this town."

"A drink's no way to celebrate. We should be thanking God."

"Is He opposed to a drink?"

"I don't know," she said.

"He's opposed to drunkenness and riotous living. That's what I believe."

His grin was infectious. Here was Truman Jackson, making light of a menace that threatened to put him in jail, destroy their ranch, and leave her and their children homeless and starving. She absorbed all that, this reckless mood at the most somber juncture of their lives, and wondered about it.

No matter what happened, she knew she would never turn back. She had put the rowdy boarding-house behind her, put her mother's loose conduct behind her, put her cynicism and fear and bitterness behind her. She had children to love and nurture, and she would do that, somehow, whether

Jackson was at her side, or in a Wyoming prison. She had found a stronger self, just as Truman had, through trial and error.

They arrived at the ranch late that day, just as the heat climaxed. Truman led the dray to the watering trough, wiped it down, and turned it loose in the paddock. She carried crates of groceries inside, found the children waiting peacefully for her to begin a supper, and put them to work at once, hauling in the supplies and setting the table.

The Old Crow vanished into a cupboard.

Later, when her sons and daughter had gone to bed, the sons sharing a loft, her daughter in a hastily built addition off the kitchen, Gracie dried the last dish, threw the water onto some withered hollyhocks outside, and waited. She wondered whether on this night Truman Jackson would begin a long fall, down and ever down, and destroy himself—and wound his family. Or whether some spirits would simply lift him out of his desperation, and make his life a little easier. She did not know.

In her mother's boardinghouse she had had plenty of experience with drunks. Most were harmless. A few cast aside inhibitions and made lewd proposals. And a few turned vicious. She had never seen Truman Jackson drunk; and only a few times, long ago, had she seen him with a drink or two in him. He was harmless enough back then. A couple of drinks had simply brightened him, helped him lose that perpetual suspicion of others that was robbing his life of joy.

He had sat quietly on the porch, watching sundown, and no doubt waiting for his boys and his girl to fall asleep. He would not drink in front of them, and she was grateful for that.

But then, in the summer's dusk, he headed for the cold cellar in the hillside, where they always stowed some ice brought down from the mountains and insulated under a heap of sawdust. Precious ice for ice cream, or an occasional cool lemonade, or just as a treat. She watched him enter that dark place, heard him attack a block of it with the ice pick, heard the rattle of ice in a tin pail. And then his shadowy form hiked up the slope to the homestead.

She heard him in the kitchen, chipping ice again. A cork popped. She heard the gurgle of whiskey. And then he emerged on the covered porch. The heat had begun to dissipate and mountain breezes eddied in from high above, promising comfort.

He handed her a glass.

"But I don't want any, Truman."

"One'll do you good and you'll keep me company."

She wanted to nag him, and chose not to. This was his choice. He was a strong man. She would not scold.

He drank quietly, and she sipped a little. The taste was strange and bitter. But the ice-cooled liquid was heaven in her throat.

"We're going to get through this," he said.

She wanted to warn him against false courage, alcohol courage, but she kept quiet. She knew, intuitively, that keeping quiet was the best thing to do.

Being his friend and lover was the most important thing of all.

He drank quietly, sighed, rose in the darkness, and she heard him chipping more ice and then the gurgle from the whiskey bottle. She sipped a little. Whatever else spirits did, they quieted her body and washed away the torments of this long and painful day.

"The worst is yet to come," he said, deep into his second drink. "Gracie, I just want one thing . . . that you'll trust me to do the right thing."

She didn't reply at first. He wasn't doing the right thing. He was drinking for the first time since they were young and living recklessly, trying everything. She remembered what they had tried together, and smiled. Reckless young people they were, and that wasn't all wrong. But for their recklessness, they might today be strangers.

"I trust you, Truman."

"They're sure as hell going to haul me off to Wyoming. They're going to take the ranch from me and rob me of my cattle. You'll have to carry on somehow. I don't know how. I think maybe two or three years. I've got these greenbacks, and I want you to hide a couple hundred where no one'll find them."

She noted that the drink was loosening his tongue and thickening his voice.

That hour he made the pilgrimage to the ice bucket and the bottle on the drain board twice more. She finished her one drink and refused another.

She stayed with him every second, until he sighed, rose, and headed for the privy, his usual prelude to sleep. He never did get drunk, but she reckoned he had marched to the edge. And she loved him, and knew she would love him whether or not he crossed that line.

Chapter 23

Weber Heeber watched sourly as a plume of dust announced visitors that bright summer's eve. The horse and buggy materialized into one he knew, and his sourness deepened into irritation.

Truman and Gracie were coming to call. Maybe they thought a little socializing with neighbors would patch things up. But there was no way on God's green earth that Heeber would be neighborly toward a pair of ex-crooks and robbers.

Probably they would come to beg. Do a little pleading. Old neighbors, old friends, all that. Heeber wouldn't enjoy that. He had once liked the couple, salt of the earth, fine young family . . . but no longer. They were interlopers, homesteading on land Heeber always considered his own. The only reason he hadn't patented it was to save on taxes. And then, suddenly, it was too late, and a ranch stood between him and the Uinta Mountains, where he summered his stock on the lush, well-watered alpine meadows.

A fleeting guilt whispered through his mind, but he harshly set it aside. People made their own beds; Jackson was old enough to know right from wrong when he held horses for his gang. And probably, beneath that adult veneer, the youthful robber still lurked.

Well, he'd stop their pleading in a hurry. The Utah Stock Growers Association put Jackson on the blacklist, where he belonged, and Heeber wasn't going to budge.

Jackson turned the buggy around the circular drive and stopped at the front door, where Heeber sat in his rocker.

"You may as well keep on going, Jackson," he said.

Gracie looked distraught but calm.

"Well, if we can't make it a social call, we'll make it a business one," Jackson said, without stepping down from his buggy.

"I've got no business with you."

"I think you do."

"If you expect me to take you off the list, you're wasting your breath."

Jackson paused. "I don't know why you put us on it."

"You know as well as I do."

Heeber hoped Pauline wasn't listening. She didn't say much, but she didn't like the blacklist, and she and Gracie had been close for years. But Pauline was out back somewhere, and that was good.

"I seem to be under a cloud," Jackson said amiably. "Ever since the potluck supper. I can understand it. But I'd like folks to look closely at our lives all these years and make their own judgments."

"You done?"

"No, just begun. To our knowledge, Weber, we've done nothing wrong. But if our neighbors think we have, we're prepared to act. You've been saying that the red cows in our herd are yours, so what we're ready to do is have you go into our herd and take every one you think belongs to you."

"You think that'll get you off the blacklist?"

"I haven't even mentioned the list. What Gracie and I'd like to do is make things right with all our neighbors. We'll walk the extra mile. We'll make peace with anyone wanting to take us to court. We've been thinking, property isn't so important that it's worth a quarrel between neighbors. So, we'll just offer to fix things with all our neighbors, whether or not you take us off the list."

The offer astounded Heeber. He scarcely knew what to say. In the end, he hated it because it might cement friendships between the Jacksons and the rest of the ranchers.

He shook his head.

"Well, that's the offer," Jackson said. "We don't think they're your cattle. Most of 'em are bummed calves you gave us, or their offspring. We don't have sale papers; you never gave us any. And if you want 'em back, we'll do it right now. Come on over and take whatever you think are yours. I'll give you a bill of sale if you want, and you can put your own mark on them."

Heeber felt something almost suffocating flow through him. If he said yes, he'd have no grounds for the blacklist. If he said no, he'd bare his real motive, which was to drive them out and pick up the Jackson ranch.

"I'll think on it," he said.

"Well, you're the first. We'll be visiting with all the neighbors and making the same offer," Jackson said. "I hope you'll accept, and I hope we'll be shaking hands soon. You and Pauline are always in our thoughts and prayers."

Weber Heeber felt bad, somewhere between seething and remorse. Jackson had just shown him what it was to be a man of faith and virtue, willing to sacrifice material things to preserve amity and peace.

He nodded bitterly, and watched the Jacksons drive away. It had not gone as he expected. He wanted them to whine and beg and tell him how desperate they were, and instead Truman Jackson showed what sort of man he was, and Heeber hated the revelation.

Maybe he should take Jackson up. A good third of that herd was red shorthorn. Maybe if he took his, and the others in the area dipped in, they'd leave Jackson too stripped of cattle to make the mortgage payment. Yes, that was something to consider, carefully. All that was required was to break Jackson's back. Let 'em go broke and leave the country under a cloud, with the blacklisting still in force.

Maybe he should.

But he knew better. Not one other rancher in the district would claim a single animal. And they would admire Jackson for offering to let them go through his herd, without a fight, without even a question, and take what they thought were their own. Of course they wouldn't. There were reps from every ranch in the area at every branding, and every calf had been branded with its mother's mark for as many years as there had been communal branding in the Cottonwood area.

And now the Jacksons would be out there, visiting them all, undoing everything that Heeber and his association had done. He was going to have to think of something. Jackson was slipping out of trouble. Elton James gave him his money at the bank, and dared Heeber to stop him. Heeber knew he had been thoroughly beaten that time. And both the sheriff and the county attorney had chased him out of their offices when he'd tried to finagle some way to seize Jackson's assets. The man's taxes were paid, and he had nothing against him.

The miserable truth of it was that Heeber was operating like a buccaneer, and people were noticing.

"Pauline," he yelled.

She appeared silently, her solid, large, womanly form materializing in the dusk so fast that he realized she had been hovering just inside the door in that darkened house, or at the opened sash window.

"Yes, Weber?"

"Were you listening?"

"Yes."

"I thought so. You just forget everything that happened here. It's men's business."

"Weber, I think you're making a mistake."

"This isn't your business, and I will do what I have to."

"They're doing their best to be good neighbors. They're even consulting the Scripture for guidance. If you think any of their cattle belong to you, pick them up and make peace with them."

"No. They are outlaws and bad neighbors."

"Maybe we're the ones being bad neighbors."

She said it crisply, defiantly, and it shocked him. In thirty years of marriage she had never defied him. "Go to the bedroom," he said.

"No, Weber."

"I said go!"

"You are angry because you are wrong and your conscience is hurting you. We are a people set aside, and we mustn't violate the ordinances of God."

"Pauline, I'm warning you. A woman can find herself shunned . . . or worse . . . for defying the good authority of a husband. Take heed."

"We must try to be better neighbors," she said, as if she hadn't heard a word he said.

He resolved to be patient. Women required patience. "We will soon have that ranch. We'll put Edgar on it, and maybe Stark, too. I always planned to keep our children close. That should please you. Apparently it doesn't. You want bank robbers for neighbors?"

"We must be just. And I don't think you're being just."

This was so shocking to Weber that he could barely register it. She was talking back. She was defying him, bold as you please, and by defying him, the duly ordained head of the family, she was defying the most holy and sacred law of God. And showing not the slightest sign of repentance, either.

He fumed and then got the better of his temper. "It don't matter what you think," he said. "But I will remember this, and it will go hard for you."

He thought that would subdue her, and his astonishment multiplied when it didn't.

"I like them both. They are good people. I grieve our separation from them. I will prophesy, Weber. Yes, prophesy! I will speak with the voice rising in me, a voice that won't be denied. Listen to this! The Jacksons have come into our midst as the scythe of God, and they will cut through Cottonwood, dividing brothers and sisters, separating parents from children, unbeliever against believer, and when this place has been riven in two by the Lord, some will be shamed and burned and some will be glorified and remembered for all eternity. There, Weber, I have said it. Will you be shamed, or will you be remembered and glorified?"

He stared at her, aghast. What had come into her? Demons? Possession? Should he commit her to the asylum? Should he turn her over to the bishops for discipline? He could not say.

"Go to the Jacksons and be a neighbor, and make

your peace, before it is too late," she said quietly, her voice amiable and warm.

She was speaking with authority she didn't possess, and he would deal with it.

Chapter 24

Horatio Bates had not even finished sorting the mail when Sheriff Quail loomed over the counter.

"You got anything for me?" he asked.

"I guess you're looking for something from Green River. Let me see."

Bates shuffled through the fistful of letters, and did indeed discover a large manila envelope addressed to the sheriff, this one from Brand Neihardt, County Attorney, Sweet Grass County, Green River, Wyoming.

"I suppose this is what you're wanting," he said, passing the thick envelope across the counter.

Quail tore open the envelope and read the material on the spot.

"I guess they're going to nab Jackson, eh?"

"Always fishing, aren't you, Bates?"

"Well, it's a matter of some concern to Cottonwood."

"And you love to gossip. Well, all right. You can just go ahead and gossip."

The sheriff thrust the material into Bates's hand.

Neihardt wrote the sheriff that an extradition

was in transit. It would go from Wyoming's governor to Utah's governor, Orrin Mecham, and then on down the chain through the attorney general to Quail.

The prosecutor said he had interviewed two of the Dillin boys in prison, and both had confirmed that young Will Dowd had been a horse holder for the gang, and that was all the evidence he needed to pin the crime of accomplice to the gang's murder of an expressman in Green River. He expected an easy prosecution, and Will Dowd, also known as Truman Jackson, would be sent up for five to ten years.

The rest of the material was a fair copy of the extradition material.

"Got him!" Quail said.

"I don't know why that pleases you."

"It doesn't. I liked him before he turned stupid. Then he went and blabbed at a potluck supper and put me to a lot of work and trouble."

"Yes, and I don't know why," Bates said, turning back to sort mail again.

"Because it's my job to enforce the law. When I get wind of a criminal in my bailiwick, I want to know if there's something on him."

"It would seem more just to let it go. Jackson's so profoundly changed that it doesn't seem right."

"Justice isn't my concern. He can tell it to some Wyoming judge. All my concern is to see that the law's satisfied."

Bates paused. "You ever done anything in your life, some little thing, that's illegal? You ever get drunk and wander the streets and not get pinched for it?"

"If I did, I wouldn't admit it, Horatio. That's the difference between me and Jackson."

"Well, we're talking about satisfying the law, Styles. If you did do something like that, you should turn yourself in, if you believe the law should be satisfied. You ready to do that?"

"Horatio, abstractions and sophistries don't help me enforce the law around here," Quail said. "You sort your mail and argue it with your pals; me, I'll see to it that Jackson's handcuffed and locked up within an hour after I get the warrant."

Bates didn't give up. "Mecham doesn't have to agree to help Wyoming if there's good reason not to do so. Why don't you write the governor and tell him what we all know: Jackson's one of the finest men in town."

"That's your opinion, not mine. Adios, Bates. This is a great day for me."

Horatio Bates sighed. Quail wasn't a bad or cruel man, and his desire to enforce the law without fear or favor was commendable. But where was his mercy? Where was his admiration of a young man who had abandoned a wayward life, fought his way upward, discarding one bad attitude after another, learning to respect the moral and social ordinances of the universe?

Bates handed out mail to people for the next hour, all the while pondering this tragic turn of events. For Truman Jackson's courage and his love of God, he would be tried and thrown into the state pen in Wyoming.

He didn't like it. Cottonwood was conspiring to wreck a good man, a man better by far than nearly everyone in that sleepy, virtuous town.

So immersed in all this was Bates that he was scarcely aware that someone was addressing him across the counter.

"Oh, hello, Eli," Bates said. "No mail for you."

"I'm not here about mail. I want to talk to you."

"Give me a few more minutes."

A half hour later Bates ushered the Reverend Mr. Pickrell into his back room.

"It's all over town," Pickrell said. "The sheriff didn't exactly keep it a secret."

"I thought he'd be out bragging. Thanks to Quail, we'll see a fine young man be shackled and sent off to his doom, and a fine young woman and her children suffer."

"Well, that's what I'm wanting to talk about. This extradition isn't an accomplished fact, Horatio. There's a little time."

"For what?"

"Some references and a petition to the governor."

Bates pondered that. A reference from a postmaster in any small town carried weight. He had given some references for people he trusted and esteemed. He had also quietly declined to support a few people here and there, along the way.

"I could . . ."

"You and I. We're the two strongest voices. And we can add Hamlin Henshaw to that. He may be a

deputy rather than sheriff, but he's in law enforcement . . . We can get a few others, too. Truman has
his friends here, lots of 'em."

Suddenly Bates's reticence dissolved. He would
not be a coward in a time of testing and a time of
need. "I'll do it," he said, "and I won't worry about
consequences."

"I'm not going to worry about consequences
with my congregation, either. A man has to stand
up and do what's right. And Hamlin—he's the one
who told me about the extradition—he'll do it. And
that takes courage, Horatio, because we all know
good and well that it'll cost him his star. He's got a
family to support, and yet he'll do it because he
thinks it's the right thing to do, just as we do."

Bates began to brighten. "Eli, I think we can
round up plenty of people. You draft a petition,
and we'll all sign it. I'm stuck here, but you can get
out and talk. And I'll do some talking to the right
people when they come in."

"There's no time to lose, Horatio. All right. For
me, this is a godly business, something that requires backbone because we may all of us find ourselves in trouble here. Cottonwood's smug and
narrow, but mostly a good and just place. I'll take
my chances, and if I can encourage Hamlin in some
pastoral way, I'll do so."

"Tell you the truth, Eli, I'm raring to go."

They left it at that. The minister dashed out to
round up support. Bates began drafting a petition
for all to sign. He intended to include a personal
letter to the governor, too. It wouldn't be easy.

Words were such a poor way for a distant governor to learn about the extraordinary life of a man who had transformed himself. But by God, he'd try.

Between handing out mail, selling stamps, selling postcards, and weighing packages, Horatio Bates labored furiously over his petition to Governor Mecham that the extradition not be honored.

"To the Honorable Orrin Mecham," he wrote. "We, the undersigned, do petition you in the matter of the extradition of one Will Dowd, also known in Utah as Truman Jackson..."

He went on to describe succinctly and vividly the story of a man and woman living for more than a dozen years as model citizens, active in the Community Church, following the highest ideals and ethics.

He described Jackson's final step to put himself at peace with his neighbors and God above, by describing at a potluck supper a youthful life as a member of a desperado gang.

No warrants against the man were outstanding. He was being chased by no one. He took this step to end a double life and be as one with his neighbors, whose blessing he asked at that supper.

And yet, upon this confession of youthful misconduct, the authorities began at once to harass him and discover charges against him for crimes of which he has long since repented and for a life he left behind him in pursuit of one in harmony with his neighbors, the town of Cottonwood, and his friends in the congregation and everywhere else. He was esteemed before his revelation; he is still esteemed.

We therefore petition you to quash the extradition. This man, Truman Jackson, is no longer the youth who, in his mid-teen years, held horses while his older relatives committed their depredations. If you are not satisfied with this, please send a trusted jurist to come into our midst and meet with us. If you will, send your Attorney General.

Sincerely, Horatio Bates, Postmaster, Cottonwood, Utah.

This he showed to Pickrell, who changed not a word, recognizing the postmaster's considerable rhetorical ability.

Through the next day, people filtered in and signed the document under Bates's approving eye. One by one they came. Deputy Sheriff Hamlin Henshaw signed large and clear. Andy Blitz, the feed store manager employed by Weber Heeber. Elton James, bank president and employee of Weber Heeber. Each of them risking their job or position or career to commit themselves to what they believed was right.

Horatio Bates admired each of those who signed at great risk. At one point Styles Quail came in, studied the petition, and smiled in his vulpine way.

By the time it was necessary to post the petition in the outgoing mail, there were forty-six signatures, men and women, most from the Community Church.

A small minority. But the postmaster was intensely proud of each of those independent and courageous persons.

And so the letter found its way into the stagecoach, and Truman Jackson's fate rode to Salt Lake City.

Chapter 25

The news reached Truman Jackson on a hot Sunday afternoon, after he and his sons returned from the foothills with a load of native grass hay they had cut and forked into a wagon.

He spotted Eli Pickrell's ancient buggy at the house, and turned over the task of unharnessing and brushing down the big Belgians that had drawn two tons of hay down the long grade.

He wondered what had brought the minister now that the Jacksons were no longer members of his congregation.

He found Gracie entertaining the minister in the parlor. Their faces suggested that the news would not be pleasant, and so it turned out.

"Ah, Truman. I was just about to leave. Gracie thought you'd be along soon, so I've lingered an hour," Pickrell said.

"We're always glad to see you, Eli."

"Yes, well, wash up if you wish. Anything I have to say can wait."

"If it's bad news, I'll take it the way I am. A clean face won't help me any."

"Yes, it's bad. You're being extradited by Wyoming, for the death at Green River."

Jackson felt even more weariness stab him. "I didn't bargain for that," he said.

"We're doing everything possible to prevent it."

"We?"

"Horatio Bates, Hamlin Henshaw, me, and a few others. We've petitioned the governor. We've written him about your years here, your life now, and all of that. We asked that he at least delay executing the extradition until after he has a public hearing or sends an emissary here to listen to us."

Jackson felt the noose tighten. "What does the extradition charge?"

"Accomplice to a holdup and murder at Green River."

"I was that. I held the horses."

"But that was so long ago, Truman. And you're not that boy anymore."

"No, I'm not that boy."

"I want the attorney general or whoever comes here to meet with you and Gracie, come here, listen to us. I want him to talk with us. As a minister, my word is worth something. A postmaster's word is worth something. And Henshaw's word as a lawman is worth much. And there's many more. You and Gracie have so many friends. Elton James is risking his position as bank president. Andy Blitz has signed on. That could cost him his job at the feed store. I think Carter Dawe'll join us. He's thinking on it."

"When did all this happen?"

"Thursday. Horatio drafted a petition within hours, and by Friday we had forty-six signatures, and we sent it off to Mecham. You've been out here, I guess, and didn't hear of it. But it was talked about before and after church, I'll tell you. This would have been the Sunday of the church meeting, but your resignation changed all that. I wish you'd stayed on. I wish we could have had that meeting. I planned to say a thing or two."

Jackson pondered all that, not happily. "How long before you hear from the governor?" he asked.

"Horatio says it'll be fast. The petition should reach him tomorrow. He could wire Vernal, and they could send it over in a day. If he replies by mail, we'll know late this week, if he's prompt. And on matters like this, governors act swiftly."

"Fast, then. And if he sends someone to look into it?"

"Next week, I imagine."

"What do you think will happen?"

"I think the governor will send someone. He's probably going to hear from Styles Quail, and Weber Heeber, and they're going to make the worst case they can, and press for the extradition. I fear that. I think Mecham's going to listen to his own law enforcement people, and not us. If that's true, you could be looking at a warrant in a day or two, if it's done by wire."

"Well, thanks for telling me, Eli."

The minister looked sharply at Jackson. "I'm here to tell you this will work out well. It's just that you have to walk through the darkness, trusting and believing. I'll be walking beside you and Gracie."

"Did you read the extradition? What's in it?"

"No, but Bates did. They want you as an accomplice, and it's worth five to ten years."

Gracie shuddered, and Truman saw her wrestling back tears.

"That's a long time," he said. "But shorter than eternity."

"I don't follow you."

"The expressman in the railroad station, the one shot by my cousins, his fate was eternity. I share their guilt."

Pickrell stared keenly. "That's been washed away by God. I haven't the tiniest doubt."

"It hasn't been washed away by the laws of Wyoming, Eli."

"You were a boy! You're a different person."

"Not according to the law."

"Well, we're going to fight this. Horatio and I and a few good souls, we're going to take this right to the desk of the governor. We're going to talk about justice. We're going to talk about redemption!"

Jackson had never seen such passion in the minister, and he was both grateful and troubled.

"You've come a long way to tell us," Gracie said. "Please stay for supper."

"Well, I just might, Gracie. That would be a treat, just to be with you. I admire you both, and feel honored to be your friend. I hope I may also continue to be your pastor, whether or not you are formally connected to the church."

"You're always that," Truman said. "I guess I'll wash up."

Truman needed to be alone. He headed out to the pump, stroked it until he filled the washbowl on the bench beside it, and then scrubbed himself with Gracie's homemade soap. He could wash his body clean, but his past remained a stain. It looked as though nothing would erase that.

If he'd suffered any delusion during his life, it was that he could overcome his past, cross a line, transform himself into a good neighbor. He'd tried every way he knew how, and it had come to this. There was no escape. He dried himself, feeling a new tiredness that radiated from within, and numbed his mind. It was worse than the weariness of his body.

The boys came in, scrubbed and weary, just as Gracie was dishing up the potatoes. Truman tracked down Nell in the hayloft, and summoned her to the table.

After Eli Pickrell's impassioned grace, they ate Gracie's meat loaf and potatoes and fresh bread, a plain meal for a hot summer's eve.

Eli Pickrell thanked Gracie and then headed back to town, pleading a desire to return by daylight. Even now, that first day of August, the days were remarkably shorter and the nights chillier.

The children, still largely oblivious of the dark cloud hanging over the Jackson family, did their chores and vanished from sight. Parker and Jon liked to fish at dusk, and swore they caught more during that hour than any other. Truman watched them go, knowing that momentarily they would find out things about their father he wished he could keep from them, and then when school began, suffer cruel taunts. If they even got to school. He wondered how long it would take for the ranch to collapse, for the bank to take the land, for the Utah Stock Growers Association to seize and divvy up the cattle, and for Gracie and three innocents to struggle to put food in their mouths and a roof over their heads.

He could not stop it.

He headed for the covered porch, and his favorite twilight view of the looming mountains. His spirit was leaden, and he knew that from now on, happy moments would be rare, and tears would be what he saw in the faces of his loved ones.

Gracie joined him quietly and for a while said nothing. But he knew she was glancing at him, holding back tears.

"What are you going to do?" she asked.

"I guess you know."

"Yes. You'll do what you have to. When will you go?"

"In the morning."

"But couldn't you wait? What if the governor refuses to honor the extradition? With all those people supporting us, he might! Please don't go."

He really had no reply. There were things a man simply had to do. Had he come so far only to surrender when it came to the last step?

"I don't want to go," he said. "It's the last thing I want to do."

"Then don't. Oh, God, Truman, please don't! It's a big world. We can go somewhere. . . ." but then she paused. "I'm sorry I said that, Truman. We won't go anywhere, and we'll not be afraid. But, oh, my darling, my love, I'll miss you."

"I may never see you again, Gracie. I may never see the children again."

She began to sob. "I know. And they won't know you, and know what a fine man you are, and they'll . . ." She didn't finish.

"It's a burden to put on a woman, Gracie. I hope you can keep the ranch. You won't need me. The boys can do it. You just keep pressing the association to take whatever cattle they think don't belong to us. It's thievery, but so what? That's what's in Weber Heeber's soul, and he'll pay for it someday. But you'll get along, Gracie. You'll get along, and don't wait for me."

"Don't wait?"

"Don't wait for me, Gracie. Live your life, and let go of me. I was born to an outlaw family, and now it's sealed."

"Don't wait, Truman? What are you saying? That you won't wait for me?"

"I'll be waiting for you every day, every hour, every second, Gracie."

"I will wait for you forever," she said.

Gracie wept. He held her hand as she sat beside him. She had come along the same road, and knew what he would do, and hadn't fought it.

Chapter 26

In the first light Truman Jackson saddled his bay, deciding carefully what he would take. The ride would be a long, hard one. He anchored his bedroll behind the cantle, and then a gunnysack with food and a cook pot. He slid his sheathed rifle under the saddle skirts, and then he was ready.

After the tearful night, he was tired. Gracie had clung to him, weeping into the hollow of his shoulder, caressing him all night long, her cheeks wet. He felt torn. She did, too. Maybe they would never see each other again. He was awed by her love and courage, and her acceptance of what he must do. Whatever else life gave him, he had Gracie, and that was more than any mortal deserved.

They hadn't spoken a word all night. No words were needed. Through life's long, twisting, uphill trail they had entered each other's soul and now were one. But now he was going to a place where she could not follow.

One hard and painful task remained. Gracie had solemnly set a breakfast that morning, her face blank, her grief perfectly hidden from the children.

Now, as he sat at the head of the table, this first meal of the day being much more formal than usual, he looked at Nell, Parker, and Jon. They sensed something as they toyed with their oatmeal, but he let them eat.

When they were done, he addressed them:

"I am going away for a long time," he said. "I don't know how long. Where I go, you cannot come. Your mother and I have raised each of you as best we can, wanting you to be strong and good adults, capable of making your way in the world, living in grace and honor, loving God, and at peace with neighbors and friends.

"When I am gone, I want you to continue as you have. You, my sons, will manage the ranch, doing as I have done. It will be difficult. Some of our neighbors may claim some of our cattle. Your mother will be alone, struggling to keep a roof over your heads and food on the table for you. Help her every way you know how.

"I am not simply asking this; I am charging you with these tasks and responsibilities, and I want you to keep what you've been asked to do sacred within you.

"I do not know when I will see you. Don't think of yourself as orphaned, because I will be present in spirit if not body. You may suffer things in school, things that I will not tell you about now. Be of good heart. There may be cruel people in the world, but it is a good place, and you have a refuge against all slights and misfortunes in God.

"So I will say good-bye to each of you now. You,

Nell, are my beloved daughter. You, Parker and Jon, are my beloved sons. Let nothing separate our spirits."

"Where are you going?" Parker asked.

"I cannot tell you now. Soon you will know."

"Why are you going?"

"To pay a debt."

"But couldn't you pay it here?"

"The only way I can pay this debt is to leave here."

The children stared numbly at their empty dishes, afraid to look at him. Gracie sat terribly still, almost frozen, her hands clasped.

"Nell," he said, "ask a blessing."

"After breakfast?"

"Ask a blessing upon this family."

She eyed him distrustfully, and finally bowed her head.

"Thank you, God, for this family," she said.

Truman reached across the table, touched her cheek, and smiled. "Come see me go," he said.

He stood, but they sat, as if riveted to their chairs.

Then, slowly, they filed outside into the brisk dawn air. Gracie walked rigidly. He saw the invisible tears on her cheeks, the tears her children could not see.

The low sun, rising in the east, cast orange light and long shadows over the ranch, and gilded the looming flanks of the Uinta Mountains. He beheld the ranch in that soft light, beheld the home he had built with ax and saw, beheld his barn, beheld the cross-buck fences, the well, the corrals, the cattle and horses standing peacefully as the long light lit their flanks. He saw the love of God upon this homestead, and the innocence of those who stood before him, the children hurt and puzzled and afraid.

He saw Gracie, and she saw him, and when they gazed at each other he knew her strength and her strength comforted him. He unwound the reins from the hitch rail, put his left foot in the stirrup, and mounted the bay, which quivered slightly under his weight. It was his best saddle horse and would take him through hard places.

"God be with you," he said, not wanting to prolong that bleak moment, and rode away. He headed toward the foothills, through open pasture land— but not toward town. And when he reached a headland where he could look down upon his ranch and across the valley of the South Fork, he did turn and pause. They stood below, small dots. Not one of them had moved. He lifted his hat, waved it, and then rode slowly onward, climbing all the while.

Then they were out of sight, and he was alone.

Before him loomed a trackless wilderness barely known even to the people of Cottonwood. He rode an arid slope, but ahead he would find grassy parkland, and then forest, and then timber so heavy that he would have trouble piercing it. And beyond that, an alpine upland, cold and harsh, in the shadow of thirteen-thousand-foot peaks covered with snow. It might be late summer in Cottonwood, but it would be early winter up there, and he would find little protection in his bedroll.

He would encounter deadfall so thick that his bay might not be able to negotiate it, and rushing creeks so cold and perilous that he would be in mortal danger each time he crossed one. But it would be a place where no man could follow, not even a sheriff with bloodhounds. And then, once he topped that great spine of mountain and began his descent, he would be free to do what he must do.

He rode slowly up the sunlit slope, sparing the bay, feeling the tug of his loved ones and the whisper of his heart, telling him to flee home, flee to the arms of his beloved. The horse sensed his reluctance, and slowed almost to a stop until he jabbed its belly with his spurs. With ears back, the horse walked sullenly ahead, fearing what lay above as much as Jackson did. Grizzlies, wolves, black bears, and catamounts lived up there. But he did not fear them. He feared, most of all, the temptation to surrender and go home. Each step of the bay took him farther from Gracie and the children, and each step wrung resolve from him until he could go no farther.

He reached a slope dotted with juniper and an occasional ponderosa, where he dismounted and stood, staring down upon a vast panorama, hazed in blue. The tug was terrible, as if he were wrestling the devil. Where was God, and why did Jackson feel so forsaken and abandoned? Had he wanted only to take the last step, the step that would free him of his past? Had he followed, to the best of his ability, the ways of the Lord? Why this? Why was he now riding through uplands, farther from the footfall of mankind, ever onward?

He could not answer these things. He would do what he had to do, for no reason. Reasons didn't matter. A man with a debt had to pay it. All that day he struggled up slope, feeling the bay tire under him. And yet, by nightfall he was far from the summits, the alpine ridges that would take him to the north slope. He had no answers, so he stopped asking questions. He had been born an outlaw, grew up among outlaws, and that was how the die had been cast. He could not change what had been.

He eyed the heavens fretfully, fearing a lashing alpine storm, but all he saw was cobalt-blue heaven, even as the sun slid behind the towering purple facade of the mountains. It turned cold fast. One moment the sun warmed him; the next, frosty air eddied around him. He studied the area for shelter in the event of a deluge, and saw nothing. The rocky palisades that might afford a sheltering hollow lay much farther up. The best he could do here would be to don his slicker and clamber into a juniper thicket.

He unsaddled and unbridled the bay, slipped a halter on, let it drink, and then let the horse graze on a long picket rope. He had chosen this place because of a splashing rivulet that tumbled noisily down the mountain, charged by snowmelt far above.

He would eat simply. He had packed things that would keep, and that would boil. He built a fire in a hollow, where eyes far below could not see the flame, cut up some potatoes, and put them in his cook pot. He knew that there would be times, ahead, when a deluge or wind or snow would make a fire impossible, and then he would go hungry. But he knew how to endure hunger. One thing he had learned as a member of the Dillin-Dowd Gang, outlaws rode with hunger, defying it, eating only when it was safe.

But this night, still on the lower slopes, he ate potatoes, made some tea in the same pot, and then drank the tea out of that pot.

He sat quietly after his meal, thinking about his family far below. Gracie had always borne heavy burdens, but now they were heavier than her small shoulders had ever known. Yet, somehow, he knew she would endure. It might be harder for the children, especially when the whole story was revealed to them. He could offer them no comfort now, except to bless them and surrender them to the hands of God.

He unrolled his blanket, and a canvas ground cloth that offered a modicum of shelter, and crawled in. The saddle would do for a pillow. The icy air would nip his face, but the rest of him would remain warm enough this night.

Unless it stormed.

Chapter 27

Jackson slept fitfully, his dreams haunted, and when he awoke before dawn, the eastern firmament was lined with blue where it joined the horizon. The wind had shifted in the night, and eddied down from high above like a premonition.

He arose and walked the stiffness out of his body. The horse was all right, and snorted softly as he approached. This night, at any rate, he had escaped trouble.

He found more dry wood and built a tiny fire in the hollow, well hidden from eyes below. When his water was boiling, he added ground Arbuckles to it and waited while the coffee boiled. He didn't much care about food, but wanted the coffee to brighten his morning. By the time the pot had cooled and he could drink from it, he discovered billowy white clouds hanging from each peak: Marsh Peak and Mount Leidy in the east, and Gilbert Peak to the west. His course would take him between those giants, high, higher than he had ever ridden.

The clouds boded ill. How many times had he

watched those soft clouds on a summer's morning
turn into massive black-bottomed thunderheads
that would vent their wrath upon the peaks and
then drift down to the several valleys of the Cottonwood River and bless the pastures along them.

And around noon he would be right in the middle of all that, riding through the great saddles that
separated the highest mountains in Utah.

He would not turn back. Neither would he wait.
His gaze turned yearningly down the long slope to
the south, to the unseen place where his ranch
house stood, and Gracie lay abed, and the children
still slumbered innocently. He wished he could
somehow send a message to Gracie, if only to tell
her he was high up the slopes of the mountains,
thinking of her. Love itself was a miracle. That a
woman would love him, no matter where he came
from or how he began his life, that, too, was a miracle.

If she was awake, she was thinking of him. He
knew that as surely as he knew he was sitting there
beside that creek. He hoped she would be spared
trouble a few more days, at least as long as it took
him to complete his ride. But he had been a fugitive
before, and knew how little the world's schedules
revolved around the needs of those in flight.

The bay was staring at a copse of ponderosa, and
Jackson stared, too, but saw nothing. A coyote perhaps. He washed his pot and loaded his gear behind the cantle, just as the day before, except this
time he tied his black slicker on top of the bedroll.

Then he saddled the bay gelding, which trembled as he tightened the cinch, and rode softly up the long stairway to the throne of God. This time the bay was not eager, and it sniffed the air, sawed its head up and down, and fought the reins. But Jackson held him on a steady course higher and higher, and finally into timber. The bay wove and dodged, and stepped gingerly over deadfall, and when the way ahead was blocked, Jackson resorted to a creek, except that it, too, was often blocked by logjams, or small falls, or choking willow brush.

Rivers of brutal cold whipped by, starting and stopping as suddenly as a John Phillip Sousa march.

Jackson knew he was lost. He could do little more than keep on climbing, guess the time of day, and try to head north, ever north. And thus, that long morning, he and his trembling saddler worked higher and higher, topping forested ridges, plunging into precipitous drainages, piercing into grassy parks filled with alpine flowers, scaling cliffs, until both man and horse were exhausted. By midday they had reached a saddle guarded by two giant mountains. And by noon the sun had vanished behind those black-bellied clouds looming on the peaks, and he knew he would soon be in for it.

He had never been this high, but he had heard tales of horror, of lightning crashing about, berserk thunder and icy rain lashing these uplands, of men gone mad, of animals felled by balls of fire, of terror worse than the terror of dying. He paused for a lunch and gnawed on some of Gracie's fresh bread while the horse stood nervously, its flesh quivering, its head swerving one direction and another in search of unseen but well-fathomed enemies. It didn't touch a blade of grass.

Jackson calculated, despondently, that he would top the saddle just about the time the afternoon storms would break. But there could be no turning back. He would go forward, and lightning could strike him dead, but he would do what he had to do, for his sake, for Gracie's sake, for the children's sake. The thought of them filled him with longing. Would he ever see them again? Would he ever give away Nell in marriage? Would he ever see Parker or Jon begin his own family and life? Would one or another stay on and ranch in Cottonwood? Would Gracie, ah, Gracie, Gracie . . . endure?

He settled himself in the saddle and urged the reluctant bay forward, climbing again, climbing toward Fate. Who could say what lay on the other side of that saddle of mountains, if he survived this looming afternoon?

He fought through more timber, more dead ends, worked around more impassable canyons carved by tumults of water, and emerged suddenly on an upland meadow that stretched between the roots of the mountains on either side. Even as he gazed at this featureless upland, it grew dark and cold and the clouds sawed off the mountains scarcely a hundred feet above him. The plain darkened until even fifty yards seemed obscure, and he marveled that the sun could be extinguished in the middle of the day.

Then thunder boomed a gigantic timpani rumbling not far above, and the dreaded flashes of lightning crackled about him. The horse went mad, bucked crazily under him, and tried to run, but Jackson fought him back to a quiet walk. His heart pounded. Then came a seductive pause; no thunder echoed off the mountains, and he hoped the worst had passed.

It began to drizzle, and he put on his slicker. It was a pathetic defense against an alpine deluge, and he knew water would river down his neck. He watched the rain come like an advancing army, in gusts across the saddle, white walls dancing like ghostly soldiers, and then it smacked him like a slap in the face, torrents of cold. The bay shrieked and lowered its head, but Jackson wrestled the horse into walking ahead. The featureless ridge they traversed offered no shelter.

White balls of light exploded about him, the cannonades of thunder rising up from below him, snapping and crackling. He watched snakes of white light writhe across the meadow, the heavens erupt, the flashes so blinding that he couldn't see. A bolt seared close, knocking his horse sideways, and Jackson's heart raced.

He found himself shaking. Water rivered off him. The bay's pelt turned black. He felt icy water shocking his thighs and buttocks. Sleet whipped against his face.

The horse refused to budge, and didn't yield to

stern kicks with his rowels. The beast trembled. Jackson dismounted and felt good standing. But the storm's fury rose even higher, the gusts almost toppling him. He tugged the horse forward.

"Come on, boy, we'll get off this ridge," he said. But the animal froze.

Truman Jackson knew he was close to the end. The blinding flashes were continuous, shaking the rock he stood on. Soon a bolt would strike him right there, unprotected and unable to move.

He was afraid.

"I'm going to take the last step because You want me to. If I die, I'll die trying," he said.

He felt an odd peace. The storm roared unabated, but he felt himself in a cocoon, as if the fury of the lightning was distant and harmless. He tugged the reins and the bay followed. He trudged through the rain, his boots soaked and his feet numb, walked north, ever north, and then sensed that he was descending. He could not tell where he was. The clouds were above and around and below him now. He didn't know what direction he was going, only that he was slowly descending, and entering timber once again. Maybe the same timber he had exited an hour ago. But in the timber lay comfort. The winds slowed and stopped, and less rain pierced the canopy above him. The horse stopped shaking.

He continued for an hour more, descending perhaps a thousand feet. Ahead lay a streak of blue sky. He came, to his surprise, to a dry place and stopped. He had survived the ridge, walked through lightning.

He unsaddled the bay and wiped it down with the soaked saddle blanket. He and the bay were unscathed. A calmness had returned to the bay's eyes. He halted the horse and tied it to a picket rope so it could graze. He had no idea of the time. Perhaps it was only mid-afternoon. But it was time to take stock. He had walked through the worst. No mountain would ever terrorize him again. He found dry wood and built a campfire, and soon had some tea brewing. While it steeped he undressed, wrung out his clothing, and set it close to the flame, hoping it would dry a little.

He was taking the final step, and not even the mountains had stopped him.

He thought he heard an animal. His bay stared at some brush. He pulled his soaked rifle from its sheath and tried to wipe it down, but droplets clung to the barrel and stock. The noise ceased, and the bay assaulted more alpine grass.

He let the pot cool and then sipped tea. Never had a hot drink been more welcome. As he sipped, the last of the storm clouds drifted east, and he knew the sun was low behind the massive bulk of Gilbert Peak, one of the highest points in Utah, and that he was on the northern slope of the Uintas. Soon he would be able to watch the sun vanish in the northwest. Before him a hazy blue panorama stretched, thousands of feet and perhaps fifty miles ahead.

He still had a two-day ride, or more if he ran into obstacles. Then he would reach arid country, hot and naked, and he would turn east, his destination the Green River. At that point he would take the last step.

Chapter 28

Horatio Bates pounced on the letter from the governor, which was addressed to himself. He was in the middle of sorting the day's mail, and three impatient people were standing on the other side of the counter, but he decided they could wait.

He hastened into the rear office and tore open the envelope. The governor's note was handwritten and brief.

Dear Mr. Bates,
I am in receipt of your letter and petition in the matter of the extradition of Will Dowd, known as Truman Jackson.

Normally we honor all extradition requests unless there is a warrant outstanding in Utah, which does not seem to be the case. The information provided me suggests that more information is needed before I can make a decision.

I wish to arrange a hearing at one in the afternoon on August 10 at any suitable place, such as a courtroom. I am sending Mr. Markham, assistant attorney general, to hear

both sides and interview the man under
Wyoming indictment, Dowd or Jackson. I will
entrust you with the task of arranging the matter, supplying witnesses, and making sure the
sheriff and others who favor complying with
the extradition are at hand as well to present
their side.

Sincerely,
Orrin Mecham

Bates reread the letter, savoring a victory.

"Hey, Horatio, put the mail up!" yelled Jamie De-
Beers.

"All right, all right," muttered the postmaster.

The crowd had grown to six. Swiftly he popped
letters into cubicles, or sometimes handed an envelope to one of those who waited with all the eager-
ness of someone expecting a thousand-dollar
inheritance.

But his thoughts were on other things.

"Horatio, this one isn't for me," said Ruby Port-
neuf.

"Ah, sorry, sorry . . ."

Eventually he finished sorting the mail and
handed it out. Then he reread the letter from the
governor—a few more times. Yes, he could set up
the hearing. Use the courtroom. Judge Hinge
wouldn't mind. Bring in Truman. Let the assistant
attorney general see Truman and Gracie; let a
dozen good people in town be character witnesses;
point out that Jackson was wanted elsewhere for
nothing. They'd make a fine case, with the Jacksons

the centerpiece. And Markham would catch the stagecoach back to Salt Lake with a recommendation not to honor the extradition.

Oh, that would be justice indeed.

Within hours, Horatio Bates had spread the word among those who defended the Jacksons. Eli Pickrell volunteered to contact everyone in his congregation who might offer a good word about Truman and Gracie.

Near the end of the day, Bates closed up a little early and walked over to the courthouse to deliver the news to Styles Quail. The governor wanted him and others of his belief on hand, and so it behooved the postmaster to make the matter known.

He found the sheriff puffing a cigar at the barred open window near his desk.

"I know," Quail said without preamble. "Mecham wrote me, too. And I've been hearing about your letter all afternoon."

"Well, that is fine, then. Would you talk to the judge about making the courtroom available?"

"I've done it."

"This is what I've hoped for," Bates said.

Quail shrugged. "We'll see. I haven't heard yet from a few county attorneys and lawmen in Montana. If Jackson's indicted a few more places, Mecham isn't going to stand in the way."

Bates resisted the temptation to argue with the man.

"Eli Pickrell and I'll drive out to talk with Truman and Gracie this evening," he said. "As long as they're Exhibit A."

"Saves me the work."

Quail sucked hard on the cheroot, and let the smoke eddy from his nostrils. Bates rather liked the smell of cigars, even though most people didn't. He even liked the sheriff, who was both honest and fearless.

Eli Pickrell met him at Mamie's Eats at five, and they each downed the blue plate du jour, which that evening was beef stew with plenty of fresh bread to mop it up.

They anted up the forty-cent tariff and left two-cent tips for Mamie, who was working alone that afternoon. Then they clambered into Pickrell's battered buggy and set forth for the South Fork to break the good news to Truman and Gracie.

They were in a euphoric mood. A hearing was as much as they could hope for. A good hearing would rescue the Jacksons from some of the trouble looming over them, and maybe restore the Jacksons to their rightful place in Cottonwood. The diehards would always be trouble, for they refused to accept that a man could reform himself. And the Stock Growers had blacklisted Truman and Gracie, but the Jacksons would deal with that, as well as Weber Heeber. Even now, from what Bates had heard, Truman had told his neighbors to take any cattle they thought were theirs, no matter how shaky the claim. That, surely, was walking the extra mile.

They pulled into Truman and Gracie's place at a quiet time of day, when the world seemed settled.

Gracie waited on the front porch as they pulled up, however, Bates did not feel welcome.

"Good evening, Gracie," he said. "Nice evening for a drive."

"Yes," she said. Then after a long pause, "Won't you join me? I think we'll have a nice sunset."

"I guess we will. I've always admired the view here."

She smiled, or seemed to, as the postmaster and the minister descended to the dirt and Pickrell hooked a carriage weight to the dray.

"How about some cool cider? We pressed some apples," she said.

"That would be fine, Gracie. Is Truman about?"

"Well, no."

"He coming soon?"

"I don't think so."

"Well, we have some good news, mighty fine news, Gracie."

She smiled. "Let me get you some cider, and then I want to hear every word."

She appeared moments later, bearing two tumblers of the cool apple juice.

"This is just the remedy for a long ride," Pickrell said. "Well, I'm sorry Truman's not about. The good news is, the governor's going to look into matters. He's sending a man from the attorney general's office to hear us out, and we wager that when he's done, and he's interviewed Truman, the extradition to Wyoming's going to be done and buried."

"Oh . . ." she said, some odd tension in her face.

"We're prepared to tell the governor's man just how deeply most folks in Cottonwood admire you and Truman, especially for his courage these last few weeks, and your courage, too."

Bates sipped, puzzled by Gracie's lack of enthusiasm.

"Gracie, this all happens August tenth at the courthouse, at one o'clock. Now, the sheriff and a few people with axes to grind will make their case, but in truth they haven't a negative word to say about you. And then we'll make ours. Now, we'll want Truman there well in advance, perhaps in the morning, so if the governor's man wants a private hour with Truman, he can have it. We think that alone will persuade the governor that there is no reason whatsoever to approve the extradition. After that, it'll be easier sledding for you. There's still Weber Heeber and his stock growers, but he's going to find himself more and more isolated in Cottonwood. And you and Truman will be able to overcome all that, with patience."

She didn't respond.

"Well, Gracie, that's what we came to tell you," Pickrell said. "Now, you be sure and tell Truman when he comes in. Out haying is he?"

"No," she said.

"Well, just let him know."

She stood, her face a mask, staring into the rich, warm sundown. "He's not coming back," she whispered.

"Ah, Truman's gone?"

"Yes, he's gone. He's not coming back. He won't be here for the hearing."

The news sank into Bates like black ink puddling

on a bright carpet. He and Pickrell exchanged glances.

"Can he be found?" Pickrell asked.

"No, he must do what he has to do. We're here alone now. We'll last as long as we can. Until the bank forecloses."

A dozen questions teemed in Bates's mind, but he found the grace not to ask them. So Truman Jackson had fled. He had lived a remarkable life, changed himself heroically, only to falter at the final step. Sorrow crept through Bates.

They left Gracie on the porch in the gathering dusk, clambered into the buggy, and drove down the long dark road to Cottonwood, each steeped in grief. The hearings would be a disaster. The governor's man would return to Salt Lake and recommend that the extradition proceed.

"He came so far. He is the finest example I've ever seen, in all my ministry, of a man born in dark circumstance lifting himself out of trouble," Pickrell said. "He may have failed this last step, and fled the law and all who love him, but he is still a fine man, one of the finest I've ever known. Maybe some time in the future, he will overcome this last weakness."

"Amen to that," Bates said.

Chapter 29

The news eddied through Cottonwood like the first storm of winter, and reached Weber Heeber's ears at the bank. He listened impassively, while Elton James described Jackson's flight.

"I'm saddened," James said. "The man tried as hard as he could, only to falter just short of the mark."

Heeber considered matters carefully. "Where is Jackson now?"

"No one knows. He fled the country. In a way, I don't blame him. He tried to do what was good and right, and the whole world turned against him."

"Well, he'll be in touch with Gracie. All we have to do is get Bates to watch the mails and tell us."

"Horatio Bates has been one of Jackson's most ardent defenders, Weber."

"All right. A man sneaks back home now and then. We'll keep a watch. I'll put some of my hands on it."

"Why does it matter to you, Weber?"

"Jackson is trouble, that's why."

He didn't tell James that he feared that Jackson would try to drive his cattle, a few at a time, to some market outside the state, and thus frustrate Heeber's plans.

Heeber was not surprised at the mixed and tangled emotions that welled through him. He wanted that ranch, and exulted that soon he would have it. Gracie could never make the mortgage payment due October first. And once the bank took the ranch, he could buy it for the price of the unpaid balance, and have the ranch he wanted, stretching from the outskirts of Cottonwood clear into the Uinta Mountains.

But his exultation was tinged with other feelings. Pauline, at bottom, had touched him deeply with her prophecy and with her frank disapproval of his conduct. Her sudden transformation from dutiful wife to pillar of independence had shocked him, and once his anger dissolved, he grudgingly acknowledged that she spoke with the tongue of an angel. He felt ashamed of what he was doing. In fact, Jackson had almost proved himself to be the finer man; would have, if he hadn't fled the tightening noose of the law at the last moment. Oddly, Jackson's flight disappointed him. The former outlaw had clay feet after all.

Disappointment, guilt, exultation, gloating, remorse, anger, all bedeviled his mind, and he scarcely knew from one hour to the next what sort of mood he would be in. What troubled him most was his relation to God, in whom he believed devoutly. He could see his own injustice as well as Pauline could, but he was powerless to stop it, powerless to let his conscience govern him.

Still, in October he would have that fine ranch, well developed by Truman Jackson and his family. In October he could add fifty percent more livestock, and cut his costs dramatically because he would have better hay supplies.

"Elton," he said, "Gracie won't be able to hold out. I want you to foreclose swiftly if she doesn't make the payment on October first. If there is a remote chance, we could wait a few days. But there's no chance."

James met his gaze. "Gracie could make that payment if she could ship cattle. It would be neighborly if you persuaded the stock growers to call off the dogs. It would be even more neighborly if you sent your crew over there to help her round up a sale herd and helped her ship it."

Heeber stood, shocked. The employee was rebuking the owner. He might be president of the bank, but Heeber owned it, and now there was this rebuke lying between them.

"Do as I say," Heeber said roughly. "Jackson's getting what is coming to him."

"Are you sure? Weber, that man came to you and other ranchers in the area and invited them to take any cattle they thought were theirs. He wanted his neighbors to trust him. He was telling them that material gain was less important to him than his good name. None took him up on it. Not even you, I've heard."

"The association will confiscate his stolen cattle when Gracie throws in the towel, and I have no say over it."

"I think you do."

Heeber fumed. "Do as I say. I will put it in writing so there will be no question before the board. Foreclose on October the second."

He stalked out of the bank, fearing he would lose his temper.

The tumult continued all the way to his ranch, but as he approached his turnoff, and the formidable Pauline, he paused. Yes! Be magnanimous!

He continued on the dusty road until he turned off at the Jackson ranch. The place lay quietly in the August sun, as if uninhabited. Maybe he could brighten Gracie's day, and maybe find out a few things, too. He had a way of eliciting information, which had been handy all his life.

He found no one at home, and wondered for a moment whether the entire family had decamped. But then he spotted Gracie and all her children down the slope in the bottoms, cultivating their garden. Of course. They would need food soon enough, lacking the cash to buy any.

"Halloo," he cried from the bluff. They stared up at him, and he negotiated the steep path downward to the widening of the valley floor, where the Jacksons grew tomatoes, beans, potatoes, corn, and other vegetables.

They stared somberly at him, resting on their hoes. Nell held a bucket. She had been pouring river water over the parched plants. The boys had been weeding and culling.

"What do you want, Mr. Heeber?" Gracie asked, her voice distant and glacial.

"Well, I stopped to see how you're doing. Just a neighborly visit."

Gracie started to respond, but suddenly fell silent.

"In fact," he said, bridging the painful silence, "I thought I'd make sure you're not lacking anything. How are you fixed?"

"We will make do with what we have."

"I mean, staples. How are you fixed for flour? For sugar?"

Gracie didn't respond.

"Well, I'm going to bring some over. Just doing what a neighbor should do."

"Are you?"

"Well, you know how much Pauline loves you, and she's put it to me. Go help those Jacksons, so I nigh decided to do that. Now, if you're needing anything, anything at all . . ."

"Anything we need is not what you can supply, Mr. Heeber. The things we need are the trust and esteem of our neighbors, forgiveness for any wrongs, and their welcoming of us in their homes. If you would offer us that, we would be pleased. If you would offer your prayers for us, we would be especially pleased."

Heeber felt as if worms were crawling through him.

"Say, maybe you could use some help. I can put

some of my hands on here, if something needs doing."

"So the place will be in good shape when . . . you foreclose?"

"Well, there's that, and there's being a neighbor."

She seemed so solemn, so worn out, so unlike the vibrant young woman she had been only weeks before.

"There is something you can do," she said. "We have a yearling heifer with a broken leg I want to slaughter. Truman always did that. It is something for men, not boys, to do. My boys lack the skills and also the years. If your men would do that, and share the meat with us—you keep most of it because our portion will spoil, even in the icehouse—I would be grateful."

"Consider it done. I'll send Alvin and Rollo over to load her up."

"She's in the pen."

"You'll have meat, Gracie. Count on old Weber. You'll not starve here."

"Thank you. And after here?"

"Well, I'll do what I can," he said. "You hear anything from Jackson?"

She shook her head.

"Back to Montana, I suppose."

She shook her head.

"He's a good man, tried hard. Sorry about all that."

She stared at him.

"Maybe he'll find some place and call for you.

Then you can start over, maybe in Arizona Territory, someplace like that."

"He's not going there."

Well, he thought, that was one small piece of information. "Lots of places to start over. California's big and there's land. Oregon, even Nevada."

"Where he's going, Mr. Heeber, we cannot follow."

That puzzled him. "No sense in it," he said. "A family needs to stay together."

"Jackson and I are together, with our children, in all the important ways."

The way she said it shot lances through him. He had never heard that tone, that sorrow, that beauty, that love, in a human voice, in all his many years.

"Yes," he said. He knew he was in the presence of something so profoundly sweet and resigned and tender that he could scarcely fathom it. She was a saint. He sensed it, sensed her beauty and spirit, and knew she was larger than he could ever hope to be.

His need to flee was overwhelming, so he scrambled up the steep pathway, only too glad to escape that desolate stare. What madness had driven him down there, anyway?

He examined the yearling, a spindly black and white that stood on three legs, head bowed in pain. Not much meat. But he would send the boys over.

He rode home dourly, his soul as much awash in turmoil as when he rode into the Jackson place. It had all been a foolish notion. Let the hard things happen.

He would tell Pauline of his visit, his offer, his kindness, but he knew what her response would be. She would shake her head, and indict him with a stare.

He wondered if he could ever get used to that.

Chapter 30

Truman Jackson fought his way down the north slope of the Uintas, often unable to see twenty yards ahead. Sometimes he got off the bay, wrestled deadfall out of the way, and rode ahead. Other times he simply led the horse around obstacles, dodging low-hanging limbs. Then the forest thinned and he glimpsed a vast, arid, brown land below, rough and geologically complex, with the snowcapped ridges of distant mountains lost in the haze. But he was not going that far. His destination was much closer.

He hastened downslope because his food was low and he would be entirely out of it in one more day. He might hunt, but game was scarce in the mountains, and butchering it would only slow him down. So he worked his way relentlessly, not quitting until it was too black to see anything. He built a small fire well hidden from prying eyes, and ate another meal of oatmeal and tea. Tomorrow, somehow, he would be there.

Even before dawn he was packing his meager supplies and riding downward, just as soon as the dusk light permitted. The temperatures had increased, and he knew that once he was out upon that arid, blazing, treeless waste of brown rock and scarce bunchgrass, he would suffer.

He wondered what his fate would be. In a way, it wouldn't matter. He would do what he had to do, take the last step regardless of the dictates of common sense. A man could choose his path, and he could choose to do the things that would make him a true man and not just another mortal hoping to become one.

All that hot and cloudless August day he rode down long, dry ridges, or along inhospitable valleys. He had been in this country once before, long ago, but remembered none of it. Mostly, he had covered it at night, following along with the others. Somewhere he had crossed the line, and left Utah behind him, perhaps forever.

His thoughts drifted constantly to Gracie and his children, and then he would be filled with sorrow. But there was nothing he could do to change things, and Gracie wouldn't want him to.

He worried about water, seeing none, but kept on. He would keep on until he dropped. He felt the bay weary under him. The gelding had weakened after days of brutal travel, and needed a good rest and some grain. By midday the sun blistered him, and he considered finding shade, but something drove him onward.

An hour later, improbably, he climbed a long slope and discovered the Union Pacific rails, threads of silver that linked the coasts of America.

The smell of creosote boiling up from the sun-hammered cross ties reached his nostrils. He turned east. Once a freight train hammered by, but mostly his long journey was marked by silence. It was too hot even for soaring raptors. But he continued.

Then, ahead, he spotted a greener lowland, a river bottom vegetated and pleasant, surrounded by stark slopes and looming rock. He had arrived, after five hard days, at his destination. Two miles farther on he crossed a rude bridge over the slow-moving, silvery Green River, and rode into the county seat of Green River, remembering little of it. Low, crude buildings lined unpaved streets. A few cottonwoods gave respite from the sun and solaced the people of this place. The town baked in the heat, the hot air shimmering every structure until it danced. The houses were little more than shacks in this stretch of town, though he knew that handsomer ones stood farther away from the tracks. He watered the bay at a trough in a stockyard at the gray railroad station, and washed the trail grit from his face. He had not seen that station by day, but knew it well enough.

He paused, after he had refreshed himself, to remember. He had held the horses a hundred yards distant from the station, under one of those cottonwoods, invisible in the night. The gang had boldly waited for the arrival of the westbound, at eleven in the evening, and then pounced. Two men clambered into the engine and held the engineer and fireman at gunpoint, while the rest rushed the express car. But the expressman saw them coming and slammed the sliding door almost shut—an instant too late. A bullet felled him. The Dillin-Dowd gang poured into the express car, ransacked it, cleaned out the opened strongbox, all before the town's sole night constable arrived, and then fled southward on the fresh horses that young Will had held for them.

The expressman died the next morning.

Now Truman Jackson stared at the very spot where the express car had rested, where a human life had been extinguished by one or another of his cousins or relatives. He did not like the feeling. Had the expressman been married, leaving behind a wife like Gracie, or children like Nell, Jon, and Parker? Had he left behind grieving brothers and sisters, parents, grandparents?

The expressman had died bravely, refusing to throw his hands up, fighting to protect the property entrusted to him. He had been much honored in the press. Jackson stood on the planks of the station platform, feeling a debt that he could never repay in full. But he could repay it in part.

Standing there, he rejoiced that he had come so far. He had grown up in the roughest nest a child could be born into, and had pulled himself up from it. When he was that boy holding the horses, he thought the whole world was crooked and rotten, and everyone was out to get him. He thought all other people were prey. He thought little of the sanctity or sacredness of life. Now he was different, and no matter what might happen during the rest of his sojourn on earth, he would rejoice that he was no longer that boy, and that he had found a path.

He stared at himself, knowing he was filthy after days of mountain travel. He did not want to present himself looking like a bum. Slowly, he led the weary bay into town, past a harness shop, mercantiles, saloons, feed stores, a livery barn, a butcher shop, a funeral parlor and cabinetmaker, a newspaper and printing establishment, and a tailor shop.

He found the Green River Tonsorial Parlor on a corner, tied the bay to a hitch rail, and entered.

"Shave and a bath?" he asked the proprietor, who was clipping the locks from a ten- or twelve-year-old redheaded kid.

"Take a bit to heat up water," the barber said, not slowing down. "And ten minutes to fix up Danny here."

Jackson nodded. "All right, start the water and save my place. I'm going to buy a shirt."

"Long ride, eh?"

"The longest and hardest of my life. Say, where's the courthouse?"

"Two blocks east, one block north."

The barber was itching to learn more, but Jackson didn't oblige him with anything more than a smile.

"I guess you have business there," he said, clipping hair around an ear.

"Yes," said Jackson. "I'll be right back."

He entered the furnace-hot street, and walked two doors to Delwig's Dry Goods, and entered. He didn't have much cash, and would have to be mighty careful. But five minutes later he emerged from the store with a new blue chambray shirt, and some underdrawers. He would sponge off the rest of his duds, and that would have to do.

The barber shaved him carefully, and Jackson tipped him an extra nickel.

"You gonna be in town long?" the man asked.

"I imagine."

"Where you from?"

"I'm a rancher, south of here a good piece."

"Ah, I thought so. Well, I'll pour a few buckets of water into that tin tub in the back, and you can have at it."

Jackson immersed himself in the tepid water, washed his hair, floated away the trail grime, and relaxed for a few minutes. He didn't have much time. He toweled away the water and dressed, feeling renewed and clean at last. It was good to be clean, inside and out, truly clean, unstained, without any dark corners to hide from a prying world.

He stepped into the street, felt the impact of the burning sun, gathered his horse and walked slowly to the Sweet Grass County Courthouse. He did not want to go. Every step he took was one that would doom him. But he knew he would take this one last step, do all that God and man and Wyoming law required of him, and do it without regard for his own interest. If it required sacrificing everything he possessed, he would do it. If it meant losing his loved ones, he would do it. If it meant tossing aside his liberty, he would do it, because it was the right and good thing to do, and the completion of a transformation that had started so long ago. The last step. The hardest and cruelest step.

He paused before the small unpretentious building. Wyoming didn't waste money on frills and ostentation. He tied the bay once again to a hitch rail, and entered, gathering the courage he would need. He patrolled the cool hallways first, finding the sheriff's office and jail at the rear, and various county offices elsewhere, and the sole courtroom up a long creaking stair.

He paused at last before a pebbled glass door that announced, in plain black letters, the occupancy of Brand Neihardt, county attorney, prosecutor. His palms sweat, even though the air was furnace-dry, but he rotated the doorknob and entered. The man had no secretary or receptionist, but sat, rumpled, half bald, jowly, bespectacled, in shirtsleeves, behind a battered brown desk covered with file folders. Dark, musty law books occupied glass-enclosed cases around the room. A window opened out upon a majestic cottonwood.

"Are you Mr. Neihardt?"

The man pushed his gold-rimmed spectacles up his nose a notch. "I presume you can read?" he replied testily.

Truman Jackson repressed the shudder that ran through him.

"I think you're waiting for me," he said. "I'm Truman Jackson. Long ago I was Will Dowd."

Neihardt surveyed the man standing before him,

and laughed. "I suppose you'll tell me you came up from Utah all by your lonesome."

"Yes."

"That's a good joke. Who put you up to it?"

"It's not a joke, sir."

"Last I heard they're wavering down there about extraditing the man."

"I am the man. I've come on my own, to do whatever the law requires of me."

Suddenly Neihardt stared. "Sit down and tell me," he said.

Truman Jackson did.

Chapter 31

Brand Neihardt listened at first with skepticism, and then amazement. Here was the man from Utah, responding to a warrant, not waiting for extradition, not even trying to dodge the law. Here was a clean-shaven, impressive man who had just spent five days traversing a rugged mountain barrier, presenting himself to a prosecutor who intended to put him in prison. Here was a man who had no warrants against him, who was unknown to lawmen, taking what he called the last step in his road to wholeness. Here was a man so compelled by his obligation to justice that he would leave his beloved wife and children behind, to whatever mercies or cruelties the world would inflict on them, to fulfill what he thought was justice.

The more he heard, the less certain Neihardt was about his own course of action. He had thought it would be a coup, a great bit of publicity to jail the last of the Dillin-Dowd gang. National headlines. It would lead to success at whatever he chose to do: practice law, become a judge, enter politics. Now he wasn't so sure.

"Well, Dowd, I guess we'll have a trial," he said. "You'll need a lawyer."

"No, sir. Arraign me and I will plead guilty. I was the youth holding those horses, and if that makes me guilty, then I will accept my fate."

"You should have a trial and a lawyer, Dowd. Maybe with your record a lawyer could get you off."

"You misunderstand me, Mr. Neihardt. I must take the last step."

"Step to what?"

"To the payment of my debts to God and man. If I owe Wyoming some of my life, take it. And when I get out, I'll continue what Gracie and I've started, which is to pay off victims of the gang. I can't repay lost life, but I can repay material things, and that is what I must do. What Gracie and I have set our hearts to do."

Neihardt stared at the great cottonwood outside, watching its leaves rustle in the breeze. "You know, Dowd, if you were to change your mind, and ask to go home, I'd probably go along with it. You don't need to be punished."

"I must plead guilty. If the judge dismisses the case, I'll do that. I'll go home. If not, then, God willing, I will serve time."

Neihardt told himself that he felt like Pontius Pilate trying to wash his hands of an impending crucifixion. In all his years as a prosecutor, he had never heard of anything like this.

"What's going to happen in Utah?" he asked.

"By now they'll know I'm gone. I know that the

people who supported me will be disappointed. I think that the man the governor's sending to look into the matter has probably held his inquiry, and in my absence felt compelled to rule against me and recommend that the governor honor the extradition."

"Did you anticipate that when you left?"

"Yes, Gracie and I did. We talked it over and felt, at bottom, that God's will required me to take this final step, and that if the governor didn't honor your extradition request, something would be unfulfilled, incomplete."

"Your friends and supporters must believe you've become an outlaw again."

"I answer first to conscience, sir."

Neihardt squirmed restlessly, his dilemma maddening him. "I guess I have to put you in custody," he said, not liking it. "Frankly, I don't know what to do. There's no direct wire to Cottonwood, so I can't get immediate answers from there. I'm not even positive you're who you say you are."

Jackson sighed. "Outside is my horse. With my TJ brand on it. You can check Utah brands by wire."

Neihardt pulled out his turnip watch and discovered it was six-thirty. "Court's closed, nothing we can do until tomorrow. Frankly, I want to think this over. I guess I have to put you into a lockup."

"Please see to my horse."

"Of course."

Neihardt didn't like any of this. Didn't like the burdens the law put on him. The young Dowd was a juvenile, bordering on adult, when the train robbery occurred, and could be dealt with as a juvenile. But he didn't like that, either. He didn't even like taking this man to the sheriff. His every instinct was that this man could stay overnight in a hotel and would show up promptly at the appointed hour. A man who had traversed a mountain range five days, to turn himself in on a charge that could easily be dismissed, was not a man who'd suddenly flee.

"We'll go get your horse, and you can lead him around. Jail's in the back of the courthouse."

Neihardt locked his office door behind him, and led Jackson through the shadowed hall to the front of the courthouse. The man retrieved his bay and walked peacefully around the courthouse. At the rear, a door and sign announced the sheriff's office. Dowd tied the horse and they entered.

Sheriff Slater wasn't on hand, but Deputy Rue was on duty.

"Better lock this fellow up, Rue."

"What's the charge?"

"Accomplice to murder."

Rue looked up sharply. "Why didn't you summon me? I'da come got him."

"He doesn't need getting. He turned himself in."

"What murder?"

"Long ago, expressman at the station. Here's the warrant. You fill in what you need."

"Hey, you caught another Dowd!"

"No, I didn't catch anyone."

The deputy arose with manacles.

"You won't need those," Neihardt said. "A man who's ridden nearly a week to turn himself over to us isn't going to need manacles."

"That's against the rules, Counselor. Gotta do it."

Neihardt sighed, his mind squirming. He watched the cuffs clamp Dowd's hands together. The man stood quietly, serenely, his lips moving slightly. Neihardt guessed it was a prayer.

"All right, we'll arraign him in the morning. His horse is tied outside, the bay. Put his horse in the livery barn, county expense, and list his possessions and store them."

That was it. He watched Dowd—hell, the man was Truman Jackson now—being led through a barred door into the rank-smelling gloom of the lockup. He watched, his every instinct rebelling at what he was witnessing. Then he stepped quietly into the narrow alley behind the courthouse, feeling the clean Wyoming breeze across his face. He needed to think.

So shaken was he that he did not retreat to the Barrel Club for his usual evening rye and soda, but found himself drifting along the railroad tracks, studying the sunset, seeing the first stars emerge from dusky heavens. Normally he would be dining at that hour, but he felt no hunger, and in any case something larger and more important consumed him, scorching his soul.

Justice.

He had encountered that afternoon the finest, most virtuous, most praiseworthy man he had ever met. The law required him to put that man in prison for a long-ago youthful crime. He realized he faced his own temptation: publicity, sensational press stories, a swift rise to fame and fortune in any field he chose. Yet the magnificence of Truman Jackson's integrity inspired an integrity in a rumpled prosecutor walking along the steel rails.

He could not match Jackson for courage and virtue. But he could draw instruction and grace and wisdom from the man who now sat in the county lockup, iron bars keeping him from his liberty.

If Truman Jackson could sacrifice everything for his God and fellow citizens and his own integrity, well, maybe one ambitious, zealous, ungainly prosecutor could emulate the nobility of the man in the jail cell.

That decided, he turned back toward town, relief flooding through him. He headed for the comfortable white home of Judge Theodore Cormorant with the intent of bending the law and doing justice.

Agnes met him at the door and escorted him into the study, where the gigantic judge, almost seven feet tall, was reading briefs in the glow of two oil lamps.

"Why, Brand, come in," the old gent said. "Something requiring my attention?"

"Yes, and I hardly know how to start," Neihardt said.

"Well, then, tap that snifter and sample its wares, and it'll loosen your tongue."

The story did not come easily. It was too bizarre

to tell. He stumbled out a piece at a time, while Cormorant snorted and clucked and sometimes asked skeptical questions.

"What's justice for? Punishment alone? Or should it lead to redemption of a man? This man is redeemed already," Neihardt said.

"And what do you want of me?"

"I cannot tell you what to do, sir."

Cormorant smiled. "You are a prudent man, Brand."

"I would move to dismiss charges but for the fact that Jackson expressly asked to plead guilty."

"Absolutely extraordinary. I think this had better be a three-snifter evening, Brand. Pour another. Tell me, perfectly privately, what you would do in my shoes."

"That would require more snifters of brandy than I could down in an evening, Theodore."

"Very well. I will ponder this matter. The arraignment's at nine?"

"Yes.

"Bring this amazing gent in, and I'll have at him."

That struck Neihardt as a good prospect. "Having at him" was Cormorant's way of saying there would be some sharp questioning.

He wobbled toward his own small flat an hour later, having spent the entire time answering questions about Truman Jackson and sipping fiery brandy.

His real worry was that somehow, Jackson would fail the test, appear to be quite another person, or answer that barrage of questions badly; then a good man might languish in the state pen.

Judge Cormorant was famous in those parts for his tough questions and impulsive and unpredictable judgments. Two minutes after Jackson appeared, he might find himself being sentenced to ten years.

Chapter 32

The cruel bars seemed to choke life out of Truman Jackson. He lay on a hard cot in shadows, suffocating for want of air even though no hand was at his throat. Had he murdered himself?

He had never felt so low. And what made it worse was that he had done this to himself. He was the cause of his misfortune. He stared at those iron bars, the chipped white enamel of them looking tawdry in the predawn gloom. If this was the lowest point of his life, that did not mean that his spirits wouldn't sink further. He faced years of hard labor, pounding rock in the Wyoming penitentiary. He faced the utter helplessness he had discovered in just one night here; his fate, his food, his health, his comfort, his very life depended on the whim of others.

A prisoner had few rights. If he was beaten, starved, insulted, offended, denied creature comforts, what could he do about it? If he sickened who would heal him? If he caught catarrh for the want of a blanket or a sweater, who would care? If the stink of vomit and urine nauseated him, who would clean the cells or bring him precious fresh air? He felt lonely and frightened, terribly alone, with Gracie and the children so far away, and no defender anywhere.

So he lay on the hard pallet, feeling the gummy, unclean cotton ticking below him, wanting breakfast but unable to go to a kitchen and start a fire in the range and begin boiling some coffee. All those things were taken from him, and the most precious thing, his liberty, would soon be only a memory.

He wanted to wash his face, but there was no water. He wished to change his clothes, but there were no spares. The awfulness of this place seeped through him. The walls exuded evil; this was the temporary home of murderers, rapists, drunks, confidence men, wife beaters, torturers, berserk and violent and mindless men, who spat and sprayed every inch of this grimy cell. And now he was one.

Why had he done this? He could not answer that, but lay desolately, trying to drive away all thought, to numb his mind and body to this and what would come. He didn't want to think about it. Didn't want to remember that he had brought this on himself. What sort of madness had driven him to this extreme? This throwing away of his life? By the time he got out, Gracie would have wearied of the wait and shed him; the children would have long since reached adulthood and vanished into an uncaring world. By the time he got out, if ever, he would be sickened, his body broken, his spirit stupefied, his soul shriveled. So he did the only thing he could manage, which was to force himself into passivity, refuse to think, refuse to listen, refuse to feel any emotion at all. Let him be dead to every need and dream within him.

And yet, in that midnight of the soul, he knew he was not alone, and what he had done was something in which he could take pride. He had taken the last step. He had turned himself over to those who wanted justice to be done to him. He had tried to pay the victims for their losses, and would continue if he could. There were no more steps to take. He had announced his true name to everyone in Cottonwood, and no longer was two people, one public, the other secret. He had done what he believed God wanted him to do, and mustered the courage to go on, never wavering, in the face of dark rejection by former friends and neighbors.

The sheriff himself brought him a tray with oatmeal gruel on it, and a mug of coffee.

"Arraigning you at nine. Finish this and I'll let you wash up."

Jackson took the tray, thrust through a slot in the bars, and ate the saltless and tasteless meal. The coffee was better. Prison fare. It might keep body and soul together, for a while. In the end it would malnourish a man and kill him.

They let him wash and then Sheriff Slater led him upstairs and down a corridor and into a plain pine courtroom, with an American flag and a Wyoming flag on either side of the judge's bench. The judge was nowhere in sight.

He sat, manacled, in a hard chair in the empty

brown room, the sheriff beside him. Then Neihardt appeared, looking rumpled and unhappy; next a court reporter entered, and then a bailiff, who announced the arrival of the judge, one Honorable Cormorant.

"Everyone stand. God save this honorable court," the bailiff said.

Jackson had trouble standing, but managed it. The judge emerged, gowned in black like a preacher, looking like a telegraph pole with a hawk's nose perched on top.

The judge squinted about, his raptor eyes settling on the prisoner.

"I believe we have an arraignment, Mr. Neihardt?"

"We do, your honor."

"Bring the man forward. You are Will Dowd, also known as Truman Jackson?"

"I am."

"How plead you?"

"Guilty, Your Honor."

"Are you sure? Have you consulted a lawyer?"

"I plead guilty, sir. There is no need for a lawyer."

"But a trial might at least produce mitigating evidence."

"That is up to you, sir. I was an accomplice in the express car robbery and murder, as described in the indictment."

"Ah, but you were a teenaged boy."

"Yes, sir."

"I will invite you to explain to me why you are

here, after all these years, and what you have done
that might mitigate your sentence."

"I have nothing to say, sir. I am in the hands of
God."

"You're in my hands, and you ought not confuse
me with God."

Jackson said nothing.

"You are telling me you won't argue for
clemency?"

"That is correct. I have done what God and the
law require of me, as far as I know."

"But I hear extraordinary things about you,
about your arrival here. Why did you ride here?"

Jackson didn't reply.

The judge adjusted his spectacles. "You'd better
answer. Do you realize I can send you away for ten
years? What that means? What you face?"

Jackson nodded.

"Speak up. The reporter can't record a nod."

"Yes, Your Honor."

"Have you given up living? Are you casting
away your life?"

"No, sir. I've found my life."

"But what of your family?"

"My prayers are with them. I will miss them."

"Don't you love them? Want to return to them?"

"More than I can say."

"But you refuse to defend yourself."

Jackson stood silently. The bailiff stared. Neihardt frowned, great furrows plowing across his
brow. Jackson felt empty and sad, awaiting his fate.

Ten years would be the longest and most terrible stretch of his life.

"Have you anything at all to say?"

"No, sir."

Cormorant glared angrily, as if he was feeling robbed of a good tart exchange. Then, suddenly, he cracked the gavel so hard it shattered. He stared at the pieces, one in his hand, the mallet lying on the hardwood floor near Jackson's boot.

The judge reddened; his pallid flesh took on a furious color until he looked like a candidate for apoplexy.

"All right. All right! You are sentenced to the time served in the lockup."

Jackson stood, waiting for the rest.

"You are free to go."

Jackson stood, bewildered.

"Are you deaf? You are free to go. Mr. Neihardt, wire Utah authorities to tell them the matter is settled and to cancel the extradition."

Neihardt actually smiled. "Yes, consider it done, Your Honor."

"Sheriff, unlock those manacles," the judge said.

Sheriff Slater swiftly undid the hand irons. Jackson felt his hands fall free, and the muscles in his arms finally relax and the pain ebb.

Cormorant humped over the desk, looming over Jackson.

"Is justice done, Jackson?"

"I thank God, sir."

"You have a way of confusing me with the deity."

"The question is for you to answer, sir. If you feel justice has been done, then I will rejoice."

Judge Cormorant walked around his bench and descended to the floor, his hand outstretched.

"If men like you populated the world, I'd be out of business," he said. His hand found Jackson's and pumped it.

Jackson shook the judge's hand and fought back the tears that came unbidden, tears that embarrassed him.

"I want to dictate a letter and send it along with you. It will tell of your journey here and how this court and the state of Wyoming disposed of this case. And it will bear my commendation of you as a man and a citizen."

Then others shook his hand. Sheriff Slater and the bailiff and Neihardt and even the clerk.

"Son, I'm sorry you even had to spend one night enjoying my hospitality," the sheriff said. "I got your story from Neihardt, and I'll never forget it, and you, as long as I live."

That is how it went there. A half hour later, armed with the precious letter, Truman Jackson left these good and true Wyoming men, stepped into his saddle, and rode through warm sunlight, without a bar, or a warrant, or an impediment in sight.

Chapter 33

That fiery afternoon of August tenth, Gracie entered Judge Hinge's courtroom and discovered a mob that filled almost every seat, including those in the jury box. Even though the open windows let in hot breezes, the fetid air choked her. Doubts swarmed through her. But this was an ordeal she could not escape.

A young, horse-faced official sat in the judge's seat, surveying the crowd with inscrutable neutrality. Plainly, he did not know a soul in Cottonwood, and she intuited that this would be a fair hearing.

Not that it mattered. By now, Truman would have reached Green River and met his fate. She said nothing about that. If she had told them where Jackson was going, and why, no one would have believed her. There was nothing she could do except let this business play out. In time, they would learn something so shocking, so searing, about Truman Jackson that they would never see him in the same light again. They would learn how far one vulnerable man would go to make things right.

"Ah, there you are, Gracie," said Eli Pickrell. "By any chance is Truman coming?"

"No, he's not."

"Ah, I am so sorry. So sorry."

The minister's countenance darkened. "Well, we will do the best we can. Please sit here. Horatio and I have done everything we can. Character witnesses, and all. He'll be over for his testimony, but can't leave the post office unattended for long."

She saw dozens of faces she knew. The face that troubled her the most was that of Styles Quail, sitting ready to lead the attack on Truman. She wished she could just stand up and announce that this extradition hearing was pointless; by now Truman had been sentenced and in jail in Wyoming. But she didn't know that for sure.

The cream of Cottonwood were all present: church people, merchants, bankers, county supervisors, and gawking citizens who kept eyeing her as if she were a gun moll about to be arrested herself. Some were just curious, but she sensed vindictiveness, even cruelty among others. A few had come to gloat over the downfall of another human being. But a few others smiled at her. Friends and enemies. Sometimes both in the same person. She sensed that Weber Heeber churned with beliefs and feelings he couldn't reconcile. But they had come to judge Truman Jackson, and she only hoped she could help them understand the transforming grace that had come into Truman Jackson's life.

The ticking clock announced the hour of one,

and Mr. Markham swiftly gaveled silence upon the crowd.

"My name is Edward Markham, and I'm an assistant attorney general for the state of Utah, and I will conduct a hearing into the extradition of Will Dowd, known here as Truman Jackson," Markham said briskly.

"Is Mr. Jackson present?" he asked.

Gracie knew it was up to her to respond. "He is not. I am his wife and will respond for him."

"I see. And where is the subject of this inquiry?"

"He is out of town, sir."

"Is he a fugitive, then? Running from justice?"

"No, sir."

"When will he be back?"

"I cannot say."

"This is most curious. I have come this great distance to examine a man wanted as an accomplice to robbery and murder in Wyoming, and yet this man makes himself unavailable. Very well, then. It will be noted in my report to Governor Mecham."

The official looked about him. "I understand that Sheriff Quail will present the case for the law, and the Reverend Mr. Pickrell and Postmaster Bates will defend Will Dowd? Very well, we will hear from your sheriff."

Gracie watched the sheriff rise and address the governor's man. He did so gracefully, acknowledging that to all appearances Will Dowd had lived a respectable life, whether from fear of discovery or because of a change of heart he could not say. But the law is sovereign, and the law must be satisfied or we live in anarchy. The charge laid to Will Dowd by the state of Wyoming must be addressed properly, or others would be encouraged to evade punishment by real or feigned good conduct.

Oddly, Gracie mostly agreed. And Quail's remarks had been presented with dignity and an understanding of what Truman had achieved here in Cottonwood.

Next came Weber Heeber. The governor's man questioned him closely about the blacklisting of Truman Jackson by the Utah Stock Growers Association, and Heeber defended the ground that Jackson's herd had questionable stock in it.

"But you have no proof," the attorney said.

"Well, sir, if the stock growers waited for positive proof in every case, we all would be rustled into bankruptcy. The fact is, plenty of my red shorthorn stock seems to have been mixed in his herd."

"And the breeds used by other ranchers?"

"Well, not as I know."

"You have or have not evidence of rustling?"

"Well, it can't be answered that simply."

Gracie fumed. She wanted to tell the man about the bummed calves that Heeber had given to the Jacksons. She wanted to tell the man about the mortgage coming due, and Heeber's role as board chairman of the bank, and Heeber's hunger to own the ranch that separated him from the lush mountain pastures high in the Uintas.

Eli Pickrell, sensing her discomfort, touched her hand and smiled. He would rebut Heeber. He would talk about all those things. She didn't know why she cared so much. This hearing, after all, meant nothing. She and Truman had made their moral and spiritual choices.

Two more witnesses from the congregation expressed their unhappiness that a former train robber was in their midst.

"We in Cottonwood trust one another. We're a small community. We know everyone, and their parents and sometimes their grandparents," said Bob Sitgreaves. "Now we've discovered that we can't quite be certain. Now we lock our doors and look after our valuables. Now we wonder about rustling, and gangs and all the rest of it."

"But have you evidence of misconduct?" asked the governor's attorney.

"Such people just don't belong in Cottonwood," the church's moderator responded. "We always rejoice in repentance and reformation and following the straight and narrow, that's the Christian thing to do, but we're not sure it's right for a small town like this one. Let them begin anew in some large anonymous place like Sioux Falls or Davenport. Our congregation's been torn to bits by this."

The governor's man scribbled something on his notepad.

Eli Pickrell grunted. "There's one I didn't reach," he muttered.

A pair of lawyers testified to the value of justice that fell evenly upon all. No matter what Truman Jackson succeeded in doing to rehabilitate himself, it was up to the state of Wyoming to decide whether that would mitigate his punishment.

"Swift, sure punishment for crimes is the best and truest and most humane approach, and therefore we both support the extradition," said one attorney, Oscar Byers. "We say this even while we confess our admiration of Jackson, who has been a valued citizen here. Justice simply is the larger and more important consideration."

Again, the governor's man made notes.

"Any more speaking in favor of extradition?" he asked, and waited a few moments. "All right, then, Reverend, you may begin your defense."

Eli Pickrell was a man familiar with pulpits, and now, in the witness box, he began a quiet, understated, amiable depiction of the lives of Gracie and Truman Jackson. He described their awakening to a better way to live, their slow, sure ascent from habits of thought that could be destructive; their discovery of the blessings and truths of God, and Truman's ultimate decision to take the final step so that he could end, at last, the double life he had led for over a dozen years.

"That was the bravest act and most moral act I have ever witnessed," Pickrell said, his voice charged with feeling. "Remember: he wasn't wanted by the law. He didn't have to do this. He wanted a final act of healing. He bared his soul to the world, and hoped that the world would honor what he did and welcome him without reservation. Alas, his hopes were dashed. Cottonwood had less charity than he had imagined. And yet it is Truman Jackson who stands out here as a paragon of courage and honor. He puts us all to shame."

Gracie wished Pickrell hadn't said that. Truman never desired to put anyone else to shame, but only to heed his conscience. Just as he now heeded the hardest and most painful requirement of all, up there in Green River, Wyoming. She ached for him, knowing that yesterday, or the day before, or today, he would be standing before the bar of justice and letting that state do with him whatever it would.

Oh, Truman, she thought. Oh, Truman . . .

Horatio Bates arrived, and contributed eloquently to the defense, arguing simply that Truman Jackson was the finest of men, and that it would be perverse to send such a man to Wyoming to answer to youthful crimes, especially after having been born into an outlaw family and fighting his way clear of all its attitudes, hatreds, and bitterness.

Several others testified. Deputy Henshaw, Elton James, and much to Weber's surprise, Pauline Heeber. That created a stir. The woman was flatly contradicting her husband, and her testimony was so impassioned and yet serene that every word she spoke bore strange weight. Gracie marveled. Her neighbor Pauline was risking everything, her marriage, her family, her reputation, her relationship with her church, to speak up. How bravely some people stood up, she thought. Nothing would keep them from speaking their minds and hearts.

Mr. Markham, at last, asked whether Gracie wished to speak on behalf of her husband.

"No, sir," she said.

"But surely you can help the governor understand why he chose to do what he did. And why he is not present."

"You all will know soon enough," she said.

Perhaps it was the way she said it. Eli Pickrell stared at her, and so did Horatio Bates. And she saw understanding in their eyes.

"Very well, I'll report to the governor," Mr. Markham said.

Chapter 34

The envelope from the office of the attorney general of Utah tantalized Horatio Bates, but a mob of people stood at the counter awaiting their mail. The arrival of the stagecoach from Vernal was the signal in Cottonwood that the mail was in. And now the coach sagged in its thoroughbraces across the street while Bates furiously sorted letters.

He popped another letter from the state attorney general into the sheriff's department cubbyhole, and suspected the two letters were identical. Well, he would see what the verdict was in a few minutes.

He sold fifty one-cent stamps to Josh Parsons, weighed a thick envelope and attached four one-cent stamps on it for Mrs. Gatz, and doled out letters right and left, engaging in the usual badinage with the good people of Cottonwood.

Why was it that on the very day he itched to slice open a letter on his desk, he was mobbed? But at last, having stuffed a letter into the hands of Tammy Grimes, who had been sent by her mother, Bates found himself free. The post office always seemed lonely at such a moment, just after people had discovered the day's joys, sorrows, burdens, bills, and advertisements in their triweekly mail. The frequency of delivery was set by the frequency of the stagecoach. He supposed that if the stagecoach ran more often, his mail would be sorted and delivered more often.

At last he slid a thumbnail under the flap and peeled it back, extracting a lengthy handwritten letter from Edward Markham, dated August 12.

Dear Mr. Bates,

I am writing to inform you that something entirely unexpected has arisen in the matter of Truman Jackson. The state of Wyoming wired us to rescind the extradition of Mr. Jackson, saying he was in custody in Green River and had been sentenced.

The astonishing thing about all this is that Mr. Jackson had ridden there and presented himself to the prosecutor at Green River, Brand Neihardt. He did this voluntarily, and with the intent of letting the state of Wyoming decide his fate.

Thus the matter before me is moot. The extradition is no longer a consideration, and I have informed the governor that the matter has come to its own conclusion. I also mentioned to him that Jackson voluntarily rode to Wyoming and presented himself, an act that we cannot explain except in terms of courage and honor.

Please convey this information to Mrs. Jackson.

Sincerely,
Edward Markham

The postmaster read and reread the amazing missive, scarcely able to digest the turn of events. While he and Pickrell had waged a doughty fight to persuade Governor Mecham not to extradite, Jackson had extradited himself!

A strange chill went through him. What sort of man was this? What sort of mortal would, given the circumstances, ride over a mountain range and present himself to his prosecutor?

Was Jackson mad, or was Bates witnessing the most amazing courage and integrity he had ever witnessed? And, of course, Gracie knew all along. They had no doubt planned this together, this act of taking the final step. No wonder she had declined to say anything at the hearing. Who would have believed one word of it?

Her moral courage was as grand as his. Maybe more, for now she and he were separated, and she would have to fend for herself for many years. How painful their parting must have been. What tears they must have shed. What dread of the future they must have experienced, all to do what they felt was right. Good God, was there anyone in the whole West who might match this couple for honor and bravery and decency? They had taken the final step, and now were enshrined by history and legend. For as long as men talked about honor and courage, men would talk about Truman and Gracie Jackson.

While musing on this extraordinary news, Bates discovered Sheriff Quail at the counter.

"Well, you want your mail," Bates said. "There's a letter from the AG's office. One came to me, too."

"I already have the news, Horatio. They wired Vernal, and the deputy there rode here with the telegram."

Quail pulled gold-rimmed spectacles from his suitcoat and read Markham's letter.

"What do you make of it?" Bates asked.

Quail squinted into the window. "I was wrong about Jackson. He's solid sterling."

"Yes! And Gracie, too! She knew, and kept quiet. They made the decision. They sacrificed everything to do what they felt was right. Now she's alone, with children to bring up, and he'll be in the pen. My God, Styles, what a thing to do. Have you ever seen the like?"

"Never. And I've never even heard of it in all my years in law enforcement. That Truman . . . he's a man like no other."

"What do you think he's in for? Five? Ten? Maybe they'll mitigate the sentence some. He was just a boy when he was in that gang, and he's lived a good life with Gracie for years."

"We'll find out, I guess," the sheriff said. "I guess I'll go show this to Henshaw. I was fixing to fire him, but now I won't. If Jackson's man enough to ride to Green River, then I'm going to be man enough to admit I was wrong."

"He'll appreciate that, Styles."

"I suddenly feel there are men out there whose courage and honor tower over mine. I guess maybe Jackson and Gracie are the finest citizens Cottonwood ever sheltered."

"We should try to do something for Gracie and the children."

"Well, there's an idea. I'll think on it."

Bates watched the sheriff retreat into the sunlight. Something was happening. One man's courage and honor would affect every citizen of Cottonwood. Here was the cynical, jaded, tough sheriff suddenly willing to admit he had made a mistake of judgment, and willing to credit his deputy with the insight that the sheriff didn't have. Bates knew that Jackson's incredible deed would transform the hearts and minds of every citizen of Cottonwood.

Bates wished he could flee his cubicle, but duty called, and he restrained his impulse to lock up and leave. So he nursed cold coffee, stared at the sky, and pondered the tragic and glorious fate of Truman Jackson, who now would spend years in the pen, starved for his wife and children, alone, and all because he answered the call of duty.

That was the slowest afternoon in memory. He wanted to shout his news from the rooftops, but thought better of it. His first task was to tell Gracie. He itched to know what she knew, how this decision had come about, how she planned to endure a terrible separation. Gracie and Truman would stand tall in the annals of human history. Not one in a million, not one in ten million, would have taken the steps they took.

He itched to tell her that Cottonwood would not let her starve, even though he feared it would do exactly that. People's indifference to the plight of others was one of the givens of life. But he would do everything he could, and he would tell her so.

The rest of that afternoon ticked by so slowly that it drove him half mad. He shuttered the postal window at four, an hour early, and plunged into the baking streets, beelining toward the parsonage. Once he arrived, he couldn't find the minister, but noted that his ancient buggy was in the carriage house. The man was about somewhere, or within a quick walk. The postmaster settled into some protesting and squeaking wicker on the porch and waited.

What good was exciting news when no one was around to hear it? Bates was about to abandon the porch when he saw the black slumped form of the minister trudging along the street, bearing a basketful of groceries.

"Ah! There you are! We have news!"

The minister nodded, and Bates followed him into the kitchen.

"Here, look at this!" Bates thrust the letter into Eli Pickrell's hands. The parson studied it and set it down quietly.

"The good Lord doesn't ask so much of a man as that," Pickrell said.

"But it's grand. Truman Jackson rode clear over the mountains and turned himself in, and did so even though Utah probably would not have honored the extradition. I've never known such courage and sacrifice."

"Sacrifice, yes. Have you ever been in a prison, Horatio?"

"No, I can't say as I have."

"I've ministered to desperate men in them. I see them as they are, cesspools, hellholes, an agony for the inmates. You may celebrate the abstract, the heroism, the grand gesture, the courage, the principle of it all. But I see the end for Truman. Those penitentiaries ruin a man. Gangs rule them, and their word is law. They'd as soon murder Truman as let him live life as he wants to in there. No, Horatio, I don't celebrate this. I am filled with grief and sadness."

"But, Eli—he's done what conscience requires."

"Yes, if truly it was conscience. We're not sure of that, are we?"

"Don't you admire this brave act?"

"It was brave. And it was foolish. He didn't need to. We were all making our case before Markham. This gesture, this flamboyant act, has ruined him and gravely damaged the hopes and happiness of his children. It could even be viewed as selfish. A loving father wouldn't do that, now, would he, Horatio?"

"I think a loving father would set a good example for his children."

The parson sighed. "The truth is, Horatio, I find myself wondering what sort of man Jackson is, with this gaudy behavior."

"Well, I thought we could drive out there and share the news with Gracie."

"You go, Horatio. Take my buggy and nag. This makes me wonder about Jackson. People who are flamboyantly good, usually aren't."

Chapter 35

Gracie hid her tears. Only when she was alone in the four-poster bed she had shared so long with Truman did she weep into his pillow. It would be such a long time before they would meet again. And somehow, she had to preserve their ranch and raise their children straight and true.

She bore her burdens with innate strength, but at night, alone, these hidden burdens crushed and frightened her. She and Truman had come to the same conclusion: if they were going to take the last step, and present themselves to the world without hiding any facet of their lives, and go wherever God would lead them, then he had to go to Wyoming and face justice there.

She believed that, and nurtured herself with that, and brought it before God in prayers, and yet the future loomed so darkly that it was all she could do to smile from day to day, hour to hour. She was especially worried about her children, and made extra efforts to let them know they were loved. Truman had not abandoned them. On the contrary, he was showing them what all mortals must do to stand upright.

One day a stranger arrived at the ranch, and studied the house and fields and distant mountains from his saddle on a palomino horse. She had rarely seen a palomino, and never one as flashy as this, with its soft flaxen mane curried until it glowed.

If the horse was flashy, the gent was even flashier, wearing pinstriped pants and a soft white shirt and creamy Stetson hat perched over a thick-jowled face and eyes that didn't blink. He sat on a handsome hand-tooled silver-mounted saddle that spoke of money.

She stepped onto the porch, warily.

"I don't believe I know you," she said.

"You wouldn't. I'm not from Cottonwood. I'm H. H. Sterling, and I'm a cattle buyer. I've just been looking over the herd. Nice fat cattle you have there. I understand you're looking for a buyer."

"I am."

"I gather you're having a bit of trouble selling."

She nodded. He obviously knew about the black-list.

"And your husband's away?"

"What is it you have to offer, Mr. Sterling?"

"Well, it's quite simple. My crew and I'll take delivery on your entire herd for five dollars a head, all ages and conditions."

She knew now how this man operated. The offer was for a less than a quarter of the value of the animals. He and his hands would drive them out of state, rebrand them, and sell them somewhere.

"No," she said. "I think we're done negotiating."

"You have no choice."

"All mortals always have the choice to do right."

"I'll repeat myself. You have no choice."

"You are referring to the blacklist, I imagine."

"And the mortgage due in a few weeks."

"You seem to know much about us. Where do you come from and why are you here?"

He smiled. "I'll pay in greenbacks. Cash on the barrelhead."

"No, we won't do that, and you won't buy cattle at that price."

"You'd better think about it. You'll regret not accepting the only offer you'll ever get."

"My decision is final. I believe we'll resolve our problems with the Utah Stock Growers Association soon, because there's no reason to blacklist us. Now, if you're done . . ."

H. H. Sterling smiled amiably. "No, I'm never done. I tell you what: I'll make the mortgage payment, and you give me the herd. You can stay here until the next payment's due. Half a year."

"Get out."

"I don't think you're in a position to argue. Train robber husband, jailbird. Nice ranch. Maybe I'll take it."

"Where are you from?"

"For you, I'm manna from heaven, food in the wilderness."

He was laughing at her. She feared for her safety. Just inside the front door was the ancient shotgun, always present for moments of crisis. She stepped in, grabbed it, and stepped back out again, the weapon shouldered and aimed squarely at Sterling, straight down the barrel.

"Go."

He grinned. "Regular outlaw moll. I'll be back, sweetheart."

Slowly, as leisurely as he could do so, he turned the palomino and a soft touch of his boot heel stirred the animal into a swift jog. He never looked back.

She shivered. Her boys were out fixing fence. She was glad they had not witnessed this.

Who was that man? He had designs on the place and knew how vulnerable the Jacksons were. Was he fronting for Weber Heeber or someone else in town? Whoever he was, he had obviously calculated that he could commandeer whatever he chose, and Styles Quail would do nothing about it.

Or would he? The thing about Sheriff Quail was his rock-solid belief in upholding the law. She would think about it. Maybe her best recourse was to drive to town and talk to the sheriff.

For now she would do what she could to keep her cattle from being rustled. She changed into riding culottes and saddled her old mare, and then rode toward the mountains where the boys were stapling a long stretch of barbed wire that had fallen from the posts.

She found them two miles up the valley, working quietly in the August heat.

"What's up, ma?" asked Jon.

"I think we're going to lose cattle unless we act quickly. There was a man looking us over today. I want you boys to gather as many of our critters as you can this afternoon and bring them into our horse paddocks."

"What'll we feed 'em with?"

"We'll put them out again early in the morning, and from now on, I want both of you to watch the herd all day. If there's trouble, just come home and tell me, and we'll go to town and get help."

They stared at her and finally nodded.

"I wish Dad was here," Parker said.

"He isn't coming home, and we'll do whatever we can. You boys are doing a fine job. You're almost men now. We'll get along."

She sounded more confident than she felt.

She rode back quietly, aware that most of the afternoon had fled and she should begin some supper. It would take the boys until sunset to gather the herd and drive it two miles, but by nightfall they would be pushing the TJ brand cattle into the paddocks. They would eat late.

She discovered another visitor when she returned. Horatio Bates was sitting on her porch, alongside Nell, and Eli Pickrell's outfit was parked nearby.

"Why, Horatio!"

"It's good to see you, Gracie. I've been worrying about you, out here alone."

"I have my children," she said.

"There's a bit of news, Gracie."

"Nell, please go set the table, and include a place for Mr. Bates."

The girl slipped into the house, and Gracie

watched her go. She, more than the boys, needed a father just now.

Bates extracted a letter from his suitcoat and handed it to her.

She read it quietly, strange feelings welling in her, sweet and bitter, serene and frightened all at once. Truman had made it across the towering mountains and turned himself in. She was desperately proud of him, and sick with sadness. She clutched the door frame, pushing back the tears.

"Gracie, Gracie," said Bates. "You knew all along."

She nodded.

"He wasn't running from the law, wasn't running from jail. Instead, he had an appointment with Destiny."

"Yes."

"And you decided this together."

"I couldn't say anything."

"Of course not. You two, you both, have put the world to shame."

She shook her head. She didn't want acclaim. All she wanted was hope, hope that she could bear the long separation, the struggle to keep their ranch intact.

"Come sit down, Gracie. Supper will wait."

She followed him quietly into her kitchen, and settled at the battered table.

"What can I do? What can we do?"

"It's my fight."

"It's the fight of every decent person in Cottonwood. I don't know any, not one including myself, who has the courage to do what you and Truman did."

"Please . . ." She said it in a way that hushed him, and they sat silently until Nell showed up carrying her kitten.

"There is something you can do," she said to Bates. "This afternoon a strange man came here. He called himself H. H. Sterling. . . ."

She told him about the visit, the offer, the threats, the open disdain.

"I can't get to town. Please tell the whole story to Styles Quail. You know, I think he's a good man."

"Gracie, I know for sure that he believes you and Truman are on the square. I'll tell him all about this Sterling."

"I'm having my boys bring in the herd. We'll keep it close."

"Good. I'll tell that to the sheriff, too."

"Horatio, you're our best friend."

The eccentric old postmaster scarcely knew how to reply.

Chapter 36

Horatio Bates hurried back to Cottonwood, brimming with fire and passion. For years he had collected stories about men and women who kept their honor in terrible circumstances. And he had acquired, for his journals, amazing tales of people who just wouldn't surrender to evil or sell out their beliefs.

But in all his years he had never encountered a man like Truman Jackson or a woman like Gracie. Where had they acquired such fortitude, character, and belief? That would always be a mystery. All he knew was Truman and Gracie had found the courage and faith to become heroes. He considered them true heroes, American heroes, people fashioned larger than life, people to honor for a hundred generations.

It was late when he reached Cottonwood. He unharnessed Eli Pickrell's horse and put it in its stall in the minister's carriage barn, and fed it some hay. He didn't try to awaken Pickrell, but walked quietly to his own rooms.

Tomorrow he would try, in his own way, to transform the thinking of Cottonwood.

Early the next morning, when unaccustomed dew sparkled on parched lawns, he hiked to the courthouse and found Sheriff Quail, also an early riser, staring at the world outside his grimy window.

"You up to pouring a cup for the postmaster?" he asked.

"Help yourself. It's been known to melt dentures," the sheriff retorted.

Bates wiped slime from a grimy mug and poured. The coffee was lukewarm. The sheriff had let the unneeded fire die.

"I visited Gracie last night. Took Markham's letter out to her. Of course she knew. She and Truman had planned it that way. I finally got the story out of her. They'd decided that it was all part of the last step. If Wyoming wanted him, he must go. He'd go no matter how the hearings turned out. He'd go even if Utah wouldn't honor the extradition."

"I was wrong about him."

"I'm glad you've changed your mind, Styles. To my way of thinking, they're about as fine as mortals get. Not one in a million would go like that, turn himself in like that. We all thought he was dodging when he vanished. Instead he was riding over the mountains, day by day, straight to the man who wanted him."

Quail sighed. "It's more than I'd do. More than just about anyone in town would do."

"More than I'd do, too. I'd be at the hearings arguing that I'd become a new man. But Truman didn't do that. He didn't argue it; he showed it."

"I guess a few men do change," the sheriff said.

"God, you make awful coffee, Styles. It'll kill you some day. Either that or you'll get ptomaine from these filthy cups."

"Serve me right. I prefer tea."

They sat companionably. Bates felt the change in the sheriff, and knew that if and when Jackson ever returned to Cottonwood, he would find a friend in the lawman.

"How's Gracie?" the sheriff asked. "She's quite a woman."

"Well, that's what I stopped by about. She's hanging on out there. The boys are old enough to take care of things. But she's pretty desperate. Her man's gone, and she's vulnerable, and she's got a mortgage payment coming up. Weber Heeber and his damned stockmen have put the Jackson ranch in a vise."

The sheriff snorted. "Old Heeber. Pious, greedy, religious, grasping son of a bitch."

Bates chuckled. "Styles, there's a vulture circling out there, and it's not Heeber. She told me some fancy dude on a palomino came out there, looked the place over, and offered her five bucks a head. Five bucks to rid her of her herd. Two bits on the dollar."

"Sterling."

"That's the man."

"I'm watching him. He floated in here a few days ago, and made the Eldorado his headquarters. Has a pair of slicks working for him. Not a gun in sight, nothing rough or tough. Just some traveling opportunists lounging in a hotel, drinking in their rooms, planning how to squeeze Gracie out of everything she has left.

"I've sent for any information I can get on him. I doubt that Sterling's his name. My old friend Colonel Atwood with the Rocky Mountain Detective Association keeps tabs on his sort. I'll know something soon, I reckon."

"Gracie says he knew everything; that Truman's in the lockup, the mortgage is due, the stockmen's blacklist, all that. She thinks he's going to try to steal the herd outright, maybe in small bunches so it's invisible at first. Her boys brought the bunch in close."

"I don't know what good that'll do."

"She's got a shotgun."

Quail frowned. "That won't help her none against slicks like that. I'll keep an eye on it. In fact, I'll just send Henshaw out there, quiet-like, to hang around."

"Well, that's what I came for. I didn't come to drink this vile brew of yours."

"I don't know that post office coffee's any better."

"Yes, it is. I clean my cups."

"But not the pot."

"The pot adds character to my beans."

They laughed, old friends.

"I guess I better go sell one-cent stamps. I'm going to start something in this town, and you can join me or not. I'm going to start a petition to the Wyoming governor seeking clemency for Jackson. I think if most of the people of Cottonwood sign it, they'll get a message over there at Cheyenne. I don't think a man like Jackson deserves a day, much less ten years."

"I'll sign it. I'll circulate it, too."

"You?"

"I've spent my life believing in justice."

"That's a hell of a thing to say."

"Go drink your own coffee, Bates."

The postmaster hurried to his bailiwick, opened shop, and began drafting his petition. It was going to sit there at his window, postal regulations notwithstanding. And he would be slow to dole out the mail to anyone who didn't sign, even if his employers frowned at the idea. He laughed.

"We, the people of Cottonwood, Utah, herewith petition the honorable governor of the state of Wyoming, to release as swiftly as possible Will Dowd, also known as Truman Jackson, from the state penitentiary. We have known Jackson for over twelve years as friend and neighbor and local cattleman and believe him to be of fine character in all respects. Justice is not served by his incarceration. Therefore, we ask for clemency or pardon of a man who does not belong in prison."

Satisfied with that, he ducked over to the *Advertiser* and ordered fifty sheets printed up, each with lines for signatures.

"At it again, eh, Bates?" said old Harlan Wood. "Well, that's good. I heard about what Jackson did, going over there to make things right. I wish I had that kind of courage. I'd of run to Mexico or some-place."

Bates nodded, noting how much the sentiment of Cottonwood had changed since word got out of Jackson's amazing trip to Green River to turn himself in. That had been the marvel, the inspiration of every tongue, and half the conversation in town for days. And that is what had won over the skeptics, turned the tide, made Truman and Gracie local heroes.

"All right. Bring it over when you've got it," Bates said. "I can't escape from about noon to four."

By eleven Wood had delivered a stack of petitions, and Bates promptly placed one on the counter, along with a pen and ink pot. Moments later Eli Pickrell wandered in.

"I gather you got back late. I didn't hear you."

"Sign right there, Eli."

"What's this?"

"It's a clemency petition."

"You've been busy." He swiftly inscribed the first signature, not forgetting to call himself the Reverend Mr. Pickrell, for good measure.

"Gracie's in a bad way. The roof's coming down on that family. But I'll tell you what I found out. First, Gracie's a fine cook. Second, Gracie's a fine cook. Third . . ."

"Yes, yes, yes," said Pickrell.

"I'll tell you more of what I found. She and Truman discussed the whole thing beforehand, and both agreed he had to do it. That was part of taking the last step. If Wyoming wanted him, he had to go, no matter if it tore them to pieces, hurt his family, ruined his livelihood. She blessed him and wept when he left, and then began running that ranch, demanding so much of the boys that they're too tired to know what they face.

"And that's not all. There's vultures circling, Eli. Just plain greedy vultures who know they've got a helpless woman in their beaks."

The postmaster described the Sterling visit, and all the rest.

"Now, Eli, yesterday you were skeptical. It's time for an attitude change. Sunday's coming up. This Sunday I want you to give the biggest and best pulpit-pounder you've ever delivered. You've got to tell the people of Cottonwood what sort of people Truman and Gracie are. Who else in town would have the courage to do that? Is there any man in Cottonwood who would voluntarily ride over the mountains to turn himself in for a boyhood mistake? Any man at all? You or me? Quail or Elton James or Carter Dawe or Bill Howell? Rafael Dinwiddy or Andy Blitz or Bob Scott? You know the answer to that. Truman Jackson's a better man than us all, and it's time you said it."

"I'll say it, Horatio."

"Take a couple petitions and bring them back signed top to bottom," Bates retorted.

Chapter 37

Truman Jackson barely rode a hundred yards before he realized he was penniless, without food, and had a long journey before him. He turned back, dismounted, and caught up with Sheriff Slater in his office.

The officer was surprised. "Is there a problem, Jackson?"

"Sheriff, could I swamp out your office for a day to earn a little?"

"You're broke."

"I figured this was a one-way trip."

Slater grinned. "Well, let's see. I could let you do that, maybe earn fifty cents. But I have a better idea. You just sit there, and I'll be back in five minutes."

Jackson settled into a hard wooden chair, feeling weary. He figured that if the lawman couldn't come up with a job, he'd try the grocers in Green River. He didn't need much; maybe a dollar's worth of oats and flour. Some coffee beans would be welcome.

He thought maybe he could sell or pawn his

rifle, but that didn't make much sense. It was a way of feeding himself if he had to, and his sole protection riding over those dangerous mountains. The rest of his kit wouldn't fetch much, except the saddle, and he needed that, too. Better to work, if he had the strength left to work. Someone would be willing to hire him to cut firewood or clean a stable or dust shelves.

The jail office had a different aspect now. The walls didn't close in on him or choke his spirit. Everything had changed. He felt safe. He wanted sleep.

It took longer than five minutes, more like ten, but when Sheriff Slater appeared, he had two dollars in hand, and these he gave to Jackson.

"I owe you," Jackson said. "I'll send it as soon as I can."

"You don't owe it. I started off twisting arms, but I didn't have to. This is a gift. We think you're one of the most worthy men we've ever met in law enforcement."

"Well, thank you. I'll remember it."

"Go on, now; you've got a wife waiting."

Jackson hastened into the sunlight, headed for the nearest grocer, and bought some trail supplies. He needed very little if he was willing to be bored by what he ate.

Then he rode out of town. He had taken the final step, the last and hardest step, and now he was free and new and young and ready for life. His bay, sensing the journey home, settled into a fine mile-eating jog, and man and horse breezed west and then south, hour after hour, not the slightest burden slowing them, under a limitless blue heaven.

He rode the way he had come, because that was the only way he knew, and by dusk he was well up the northern flank of the Uintas, out of parched land into verdant grasses. He would let the bay fill himself before picketing him close to his bedroll.

And so Truman Jackson hurried home. As each day came and went, both his anticipation and his exhaustion multiplied. He would see Gracie and his children soon. And he would see them as a free man, with no sword of Damocles hanging over him.

Even if the bank and Weber Heeber took away all he possessed, he would still have everything: his liberty, his family, and his good name. He had long known about liberty and family and what they meant. But now he had his reputation as well, and grew aware that a good name is precious as gold, and the esteem of others is a treasure without price. With his family, his liberty, and his good name, he would start over somewhere.

He topped the Uintas, riding between awesome peaks, and began his long descent. The bay perked up, smelling a land it knew. Near the end of his long ride home, Jackson's last strength faded, and he clung to the saddle horn. Should he first slip into town and see Sheriff Quail and show him his release and the letter? And find out what had happened in his absence? Or should he ride straight into Gracie's arms? He was weary. Ten days of riding, a night in jail, a trial, had all taken a terrible toll, and now the thought of home, and his own bed preoccupied him. Every bone in him hurt, every muscle. But his soul didn't hurt. He was free and had stayed the course.

He chose to climb the divide rather than follow the main fork of the river into Cottonwood or top a low divide to the South Fork. He did not know what he would find. He considered it possible that she had already been forced to abandon the spread, and then he would have to ride to town and discover what terrible things had happened.

But soon he was riding through familiar pastures, his heart quickening, his throat tightening, his body at once taut with exhaustion and wild with joy. He had taken the final step, and the worst was over.

He worked around a familiar bend in the trail, and beheld his own home, the place of refuge that had been God's gift to him and Gracie. His heart quickened again. He urged the eager bay into an easy lope, and flew over the final mile. At last she emerged on the porch, shotgun in hand, and then she recognized him and screamed, and came running, running, her skirts tripping her, running to him with her arms wide.

He reined the bay, slid off the horse and ran to her, clasping her in his arms, feeling her tighten her hold on him, felt the crush of her.

"Oh, Truman, you're here! Why?"

He realized she was frightened, that she believed he had become, again, an outlaw on the dodge.

"Gracie, it's okay. I'm free. I love you. We're free forever."

"Tell me, oh, tell me," she cried.

He did, brusquely, going into detail only when it came to the judge's decision to limit the sentence to time served, and the judge's comments.

"You took the last step," she whispered.

"We did, together, and here we are. We are free, with nothing to hide." He pulled free of her enough to look into her eyes. "And what happened here?"

She told him about that, the hearing, the many people who came forward to defend the Jacksons. About the universal feeling that Truman had broken and run at the last moment.

"And the ranch? Where are the boys?"

"Out watching the cattle. There's been trouble. A threat, anyway."

She told about the visit of H. H. Sterling, the implied threats, the offer of five dollars a head.

"That evening Horatio Bates arrived with the news that you'd reached Green River and turned yourself in. Oh, how painful that was. He promised to tell Styles Quail about this man, and I'm sure he did. I don't know who he is, but at least the law knows. We've been bringing in the herd each night."

"Gracie, you're in danger."

"Not with you here."

He and Gracie walked slowly to the ranch house, sharing news, absorbing the touch of each other.

Nell erupted from the kitchen and hugged her father.

"You came home. I knew you'd come home!"

"I'd better see to the horse," he said, not wanting to. He just wanted to sleep.

"I'll make a lunch."

"I haven't had a good meal in weeks."

He unsaddled the bay, led it to the watering trough, brushed it swiftly, put it out, and trudged back to the house. She heaped potato salad before him, sliced fresh bread, put fresh-churned butter on the table, poured fresh coffee, and then settled quietly beside him, her face aglow.

He ate, setting aside the many questions dogging him. What next? Who should he see? Had anything changed at the bank? Had Weber Heeber changed?

But she anticipated him and began talking about all those things, the boys, the cattle, the granitic hardness of Heeber, the looming mortgage payment, the desperation of living without being able to sell any livestock, without any cash at all.

He absorbed all that bleakly.

"Gracie, Nell, we may lose this place. We may have to start over. But one thing's sure. We walked the last mile. We can leave proudly. We're together. We'll go somewhere and start over. I hear there's good grass in northern Arizona Territory. Maybe we can stake some out and begin, just as we did last time. We have everything we need. We're free, there's no cloud over us, and we're together. We'll just start a new life."

"Wherever you go, I'll go. Whatever you start, we'll start together, Truman."

The look she gave him was so soft and tender and sweet that a lump caught in his throat.

It was deep afternoon. He looked about him, wondering what to do, wondering whether he could endure one more ride this day.

"I guess I'd better go to Cottonwood and talk with Styles Quail," he said.

"But you're so tired. You've been riding so long."

"If I don't, I'll fall asleep."

"Then sleep, Truman."

"No, have to finish this up. Let 'em know I'm here, show that letter, talk to the bank . . ."

"But it'll be six-thirty before you get there."

"I should go . . ."

"But the boys . . . they'll want to see you."

"They're young men now."

"No, they're frightened and very courageous boys."

"Yes," he said.

She was speaking from miles away. He was vaguely aware that she was helping him stumble to the bedroom, and lowering him onto their bed, and tugging fiercely at his boots. And that when she kissed him, tears fell down her cheeks.

Chapter 38

That morning was the happiest in Truman Jackson's life. He was a free man. His family gathered about him. The sun shone through no barred windows. He had nothing to hide from the world. He felt a divine presence in his life. His beautiful wife smiled at him. She had shared his long journey, encouraged him when he faltered, lifted him past the dark places.

Now he would go to Cottonwood and try to salvage his ranch. He badly wanted to preserve what he and Gracie had built for a dozen years. And yet, if worse came to worse, and he ran into obdurate walls, he was willing to start over. He had everything a man could hope for now, the very things others took for granted, such as a good name and the freedom to be himself.

He addressed his sons cheerfully: "You just keep on doing what you've been doing. You go out with the herd, fix fence, and bring the herd in. I'll be in town today, but tomorrow we'll be working together again. You're fine boys."

They liked that paternal recognition, and grinned at him.

He saddled the bay, hoping it had rested enough, and started down the long road to Cottonwood, through a cool morning. The change of seasons was just around the corner. He met no one. As he passed the road into Weber Heeber's ranch, he wondered about the man and what drove him and whether the Jacksons and Heebers could ever be neighborly again. He knew he would try. It was not in him to nurse grudges.

By nine, on a sunny morning, he was walking the bay into sleepy Cottonwood. No one noticed. That was fine with him. He steered his saddler to the courthouse, and tied it to the hitch rail at the sheriff's door at the rear.

When he walked into the office, both Sheriff Quail, who sat over paperwork, and Deputy Henshaw stared.

"You're the last person I expected to walk in here, Jackson," the sheriff finally said.

"I hardly expected to be here, either."

"You on the lam? Hell, of course not, or you wouldn't be here."

"No, I'm a free man. I pleaded guilty, was sentenced to the night I'd spent in the pokey, and they let me go. In fact, they even bought me some groceries to go home with."

He extracted some paperwork from his breast pocket and laid it before the sheriff.

"Hell, I don't need to read this," Quail said.

"Just read it."

Quail pulled his gold-rimmed spectacles over his nose and read.

"Judge thinks pretty handsomely of you. Says no one in Green River ever heard of a wanted man riding a hundred miles to turn himself in, especially for an old offense done as a youth. He thinks maybe you're about the finest gent he's ever met."

Henshaw was grinning.

The sheriff lumbered to his feet, his face sober. "You mind if I shake?"

The sheriff stuffed his big paw into Jackson's, and they shook. The sheriff's grip was firm, hard, and warm.

"I was wrong, Truman. I always thought, once an outlaw, always an outlaw at heart, even if they pretend to go straight. I was wrong, and I plain admit it and apologize. Hamlin, here, saw what I refused to see, and stood by you. He's a good man, our deputy. When I quit, I'll endorse him for this job."

The sheriff's arm caught Jackson's shoulder and pressed it. "I'm proud to see you here. I'll tell the whole damned world I'm proud to see you here. I mean that. I'm going to patrol every business in town this morning, and I'm going to tell 'em that you're back and they'd better treat you right."

Jackson laughed uneasily. "I was just trying to—"

"Make it all square. Well, you did. You made it square."

Jackson sighed. "I may not be able to stay. Mortgage payment coming up. I can't sell a calf, much less a herd. We're thinking of going on down to Arizona. There's good grass there, and maybe we can homestead something or other and start up again."

"You heard from Heeber or the bank?"

"No, they're just sitting back on their haunches waiting to take over the place."

"You mind if I take you over there for a little talk with Elton James?"

"I was going there anyway, so come along, Styles."

They hiked amiably across the square, and into the bank on the corner. The teller stared. Quail and Jackson steered straight down an aisle to the president's office, and entered. James, in his shirtsleeves, was reading *Frank Leslie's Illustrated Weekly Newspaper.*

"Good God," he said.

"Our man's home from the hills, Elton. And he's home free, and home proud. They didn't want him up there, and decided old Jackson, here, is one fine man. They even anted up some cash to get him back home."

The bank president stood, swiftly, and pumped Jackson's hand.

"There's no finer man in Cottonwood. No finer family."

"Well, I don't expect to be here long, Elton," Jackson said.

"Oh, that. Well, let's do something about it."

"Do something?"

"You got cattle to sell, haven't you?"

"I can't sell. I'm blacklisted."

"That's Heeber's doings. It's not going to stop me this time. Truman, we'll just take delivery on some of your cows and sell them ourselves, if that's how you want to do it."

"Take delivery? You can't. You won't be able to sell anything with my brand on it. And what'll Heeber say? He owns this bank. He'd fire you."

"Well, I reckon he might just do that. But a man has to stand up and growl once in a while, and that's what I am going to do. Let's just draw us up a little sales agreement here, in writing, and I'll sign it before Weber ever lays eyes on it."

"You'd do that?"

"I'd do it. I've watched you for years, and when all this business broke over you, I wavered a week or so, but then I came to your defense and I've been on your side ever since."

"But how're you going to sell the cattle?"

James grinned. "Well, old Heeber'll just have to take 'em to rid his bank of its burden."

"You sure you want to do this?"

Elton James turned quiet and solemn. "This is the most important thing I've ever done as a banker, and as a man. There are times a man has to stand up and be counted, and this is one of them."

He rummaged through a file and withdrew the mortgage agreement.

"Well, let's see here. You owe us three hundred eighty-five dollars on October one. I imagine you want to pay off in steers rather than brood stock. That's what you would've done anyway, sent some steers to market."

"Yes, I was planning on that."

"Well, yesterday's price for steers on the hoof

was twenty-two fifty. That a suitable and fair market price?"

"I'm afraid I haven't the faintest idea, Elton."

"It is, as of yesterday. We have to deduct for shipping. This is a hard place to ship from. Two dollars a head, railroad fee, whether or not old Weber accepts them. That's what you'd pay, right?"

Jackson nodded, scarcely believing the transaction that was shaping up.

"Twenty dollars and a half for the steers. You'll want a little cash in your account, too, I imagine. Have you twenty steers you can deliver October one?"

"More than that."

"How many were you going to market?"

"About forty."

"All right, the bank's going to buy forty TJ steers at twenty and a half, delivery at the yards here, October one. All right?"

Jackson nodded.

The bank president drafted the agreement, and a copy, and signed them. Jackson signed. The sheriff witnessed.

James handed Jackson his copy. "Now, Truman, you're pinched for cash right now, I imagine. We'll advance twenty dollars to your account, compliments of the State Bank of Cottonwood, and repay ourselves when we take the shipment."

Jackson felt himself choking with feeling. "I don't know how to thank you."

"You've already thanked us by showing every citizen in town what it takes to be a man. You're a beacon and a shining light. There's not a person in Cottonwood who won't profit from your example. I like to think this is what makes the United States of America, people like you, who get a sense of right into themselves and stick with it, no matter what falls on them along the way. If we had more like you, this country wouldn't have many troubles."

"Mr. James, you're likely to pay a price when Weber Heeber finds out."

"It's a price worth paying. I've never felt so good about something in all the years I've been here. Old Weber, he's the one who's going to suffer. This whole town's going to take a close look at him, and his Utah Stock Growers outfit, and I wouldn't be surprised if someone else starts up a rival bank. Maybe I'll just do that myself."

Jackson nodded, bewildered and happy. Had his long walk through darkness come to this? The transformation of a whole town? Was there some divine purpose in all of this? That a quiet, complacent town might examine its conscience and reform itself?

Jackson withdrew ten dollars to let Gracie buy groceries, and retreated into the sunlight with the sheriff.

"Truman, you just go on out there and celebrate. Let me spread this news around. I'm going to have a good time this morning."

Truman Jackson shook hands with the sheriff, mounted his bay, and headed for home.

Chapter 39

The news filtered and sifted its way into Weber Heeber's ears. What had seemed simple before now turned into a Gordian knot. He had put Jackson on the blacklist, so he would default on his mortgage payment. Then Jackson would have to foreclose. Heeber could then buy the ranch from his own bank for pennies on the dollar and pick up Jackson's unmarketable cattle in the process. In the end the ranch that stretched from the outskirts of Cottonwood deep into the mountains would be his.

He liked Jackson, and that was the trouble. When Jackson saddled up and rode clear over the Uintas to Green River and turned himself in, Heeber admired and cursed the man. Admired him because it was a courageous thing, and cursed him because it weakened the case for a blacklisting.

Wasn't it enough that the Jacksons had come and offered Heeber any cows they thought were theirs, making the same offer to every other rancher in the valley? That was a spiritual act, but it undermined the case for a blacklist, and that maddened him. It was enough to make a good churchman, like Hee-

ber, turn to drink. Which of course he would never
do, unless Jackson drove him to it.

And now this. Jackson was back. They'd freed
him in Wyoming and commended his courage.
Now Jackson could take control of his ranch again.
Not that Gracie did poorly. Spunky gal, just as big-
souled as Truman. But that spelled trouble. Both
she and Jackson knew how to fight.

Yet that was only part of it. His own Pauline, of
all people, had reared up, defied him, defied husband and church and state, and announced herself
in favor of the Jacksons, telling Weber to straighten
up. And she'd been telling him plenty of other
things, too, until he was ready to excommunicate
her. However, she was right, which angered him
even more because that meant he was wrong and
his authority was no good.

Irritably he harnessed his buggy and whipped
his trotter into town. It was time to find out everything he could and put a stop to Jackson's triumph.
He pulled his sweating trotter to a walk to cool him
down, and then parked right in front of the State
Bank of Cottonwood, in his usual spot. He eyed the
stone facade appreciatively. Solid bank in a solid
town, run cautiously and with due regard for
everyone who'd ever put a nickel into an account
there. His bank. He owned ninety percent of it, and
the directors owned the rest.

He walked imperially through the bank, making
waves, expecting the hush that always accompa-
nied his grand entrances. By all the saints, he ruled
with a firm but easy hand there.

Elton James welcomed him oddly, with a peculiar animation, and bade him sit down.

"You'll want to be sitting," he said.

"I want to know about Jackson. Everything. The whole town's talking about nothing else."

"He came here yesterday, along with the sheriff. I was mighty glad to see him back."

Heeber glowered. "And then what?"

"I did a deal."

Heeber stared unblinking.

"We negotiated a contract. We're accepting his cattle at market price in lieu of cash payment."

"What?"

"Forty market steers at twenty dollars and a half, to be delivered at the yards October first."

"Are you mad?"

James smiled. "It's our policy to help people meet their mortgage payments every way we reasonably can. Your own rule."

"What? What?"

"We're committed, Weber. Signed by an authorized bank officer and witnessed by Sheriff Quail. We'll sell the cattle."

"But the blacklist."

"When did that ever apply to reputable banks? You could buy the cattle, you know."

Weber Heeber howled. The groan crescendoed higher and higher, rattling the chandelier, echoing down the hall and into the lobby, scraping dust off the marble.

"You betrayed me."

"No, I did what's right. Funny thing, Weber.

Jackson's taught us a few things about honor and integrity. I came to realize I was less virtuous than I'd supposed. Made me think. Made me act, too. It's the finest thing I've ever done."

"I'll see to your resignation, that's what. I'll present this to the board."

Elton James shrugged. "That's fine. I'll start a new bank. In fact, we'll walk away with all the business. People don't like what you've done to the Jacksons. You can either keep me on and let me operate the right way, the proper way, or you can boot me out. But if you do, this palace of marble and granite's gonna collapse into rubble."

Heeber gawked at the man, at once admiring and hating him.

"I'm not done with you. I'll have my way. I'll dock your salary. I'll bring suit. Who owns this bank? I do. Whose direction do you follow? Mine. I expect unquestioning obedience to my directives. I despise betrayal, sneaking around behind my back, treachery, disobedience, dishonor . . ."

The president of the bank was smiling. "I'd do it again," he said. "And I'll tell you something else. If your Utah Stock Growers continue to keep the Jacksons blacklisted, half the town would ante up the funds to make that payment. I know. I've been talking all morning with merchants. There's not a one doesn't feel bad about all this. Talked with half the county supervisors, too. Not a one would go along with you and your schemes to grab a man's ranch. You're out of step, Weber. For the sake of your soul, change your ways. For a start, tell your stock growers to lift that phony blacklist. There never was a shred of evidence, except in your wormy brain."

Weber Heeber, employer, deacon, and leading light, was speechless.

He tasted gall and wormwood in his mouth, and spat.

"You'll hear from me," he said, and staggered outside, wondering if he was about to succumb to a heart attack. But he didn't. He stood in the August heat, radiating malice. A woman with a perambulator gave wide berth. Jackson had outwitted him. The man had a cunning criminal mind, and had outflanked and outfoxed him. No, that wasn't right. That was all wrong. He glared imperiously at passersby, and stepped into his buggy. The heat had scorched the quilted black leather seat.

"Ow!" he said, and slapped the lines over the croup of his snoozing trotter. His buggy lurched, and he steered straight up Utah Avenue, like a devil's plow curling the town into halves.

He reached his ranch house at noon, and put the horse out on pasture without watering or brushing it.

Pauline was waiting for him in the cool shadows, with a meal that had miraculously materialized as he drove down the lane.

"Well?" she asked gently.

"It's none of your business."

"And I'm none of your wife."

"What? What? I'll have you before the bishop."

"I will do what I will do, and go where I will go, and sing the songs of God as I will."

He sucked buttermilk and stabbed at johnny-cakes and pondered this amazing turn of events. She'd become a rebel, and she needed to be driven out with whips and thorns. Devil take her.

"While you were gone, I received Gracie. We had a very pleasant visit," she said.

"In my house?"

"In this house."

"She's turned your mind against me."

"She and Truman have been fine neighbors."

"They stole cattle!"

"Only in your imagination. You must remove them from the blacklist, and you must drive over and apologize to them for all the misery you've brought them."

"I won't. I refuse. I don't hear a word you're saying."

"It's time for Weber Heeber to become a good neighbor again. You were once, before Truman Jackson spoke from the center of his soul at a potluck dinner last spring. He told of his imperfections and his efforts to erase them, and his desire to make himself whole. And you turned on him, like a thief in an alley, and struck."

"You are saying this in my house. I forbid it!"

"Go to them and make peace and restore the bonds we enjoyed before that devil Beelzebub captured you."

Heeber glared, threw his johnnycakes to the floor, and stomped to the kitchen door.

"Get this straight. I will never demean myself. I will never humble myself. I will never crawl like some lickspittle and beg the apologies of that robber and killer. I'll never speak to you again, or to that perfidious Elton James. I'll never drive to Cottonwood again and listen to those sniveling vultures. I'll do what I must. I'll never tell the stock growers to prune their blacklist. I'd die first!"

He stood at the door, glowering.

The bed beckoned. That's what he would do. He would go to bed. Whenever he was out of bed, his life ran to miseries. If he stayed in bed, he wouldn't have to demean himself. He clambered into the marital room, and closed the door.

He stayed there that day, and the next. Pauline brought him food and drink. But he refused to step out of bed, and knew he would never leave that bed. He'd die in that bed before he would apologize to anyone, or demean himself, or retreat.

And so the weeks drifted by, and Pauline ran the ranch, and one of his three daughters and two of his four sons, along with their spouses, returned to the ranch and helped. He stayed in bed because that was the only place in the universe where he could be without changing one iota, one particle, of his nature. And he slept and watched the sun come and go and cursed God and kept himself aloof and would not talk to anyone.

Chapter 40

And so it came to pass that the Jacksons became honored citizens of Cottonwood, esteemed by neighbors and friends, trusted by all. Truman Jackson's word was inviolate, and his integrity was never questioned. He possessed a good name, that greatest treasure.

He thought often about the long string of events that had led him to his joyous estate. What had led him and Gracie along the right path? The only path? At first there had been only the desire to flee, to hide a past. But then they had discovered that the lives of ordinary, law-abiding people were generally happier and more serene and more fulfilling than his, or those of his outlaw clan.

Joining a church had helped them understand not only the moral law, but also the larger law of love. It was only when they put their faith to the test, and admitted to an outlaw past, that they faced the last and most formidable obstacles.

He thought often of lecturing his children about the mistakes and successes of his own life, but he didn't. They would absorb his and Gracie's exam-

ple of the art of living. They could see with their
own eyes the result of honor and honesty, and over
the years he watched them spring up into strong,
self-possessed, honorable young people. If he and
Gracie had failed to take that final step and face the
consequences, their children would not have been
so well prepared to enter their own adult lives. Jon
planned to ranch with his father, but Parker
dreamed of other things, and distant shores, and
Truman and Gracie waited to see what their
younger son would do with his life.

They never did escape the blacklist imposed by
the Utah Stock Growers, but it made no difference.
Elton James, at the bank, was their ferocious defender and invited every passing range detective
into his office for a blistering lecture. The railroads
eventually shipped Jackson cattle. Their neighbors
defended the Jacksons so stoutly that any detective
looking into the matter simply concluded that the
anti-rustling measures of the Utah cattlemen were
sometimes unjust and wrong.

The Jacksons often visited the Heeber ranch, and
were always graciously received by Pauline. But
Weber had retired to his bed, turning his back to
the world, and that bedroom door remained closed
for many years.

In the middle of many a night, Truman Jackson
arose, padded to the window to stare at the heavens, and affirmed a profound truth. Even if he had
languished for years in a Wyoming jail, even if the
ranch had been taken away, even if Gracie and the
children had suffered poverty and sorrows, even if

all of Cottonwood had turned its back on them, he would have persevered, taken that final step and borne the consequences, and would have been made whole, along with his family.